south side sports

In the Paint

Jeff Rud

ORCA BOOK PUBLISHERS

National Library of Canada Cataloguing in Publication Data

Rud, Jeff, 1960-
In the paint / Jeff Rud.

(South Side sports)
ISBN 1-55143-337-0

I. Title. II. Series: Rud, Jeff, 1960- . South Side sports.

PS8635.U32I5 2005   jC813'.6   C2005-901413-X

Summary: Twelve-year-old Matt Hill struggles to make the
basketball team in his new school while keeping out of trouble.

First published in the United States, 2005
Library of Congress Control Number: 2005922924

Orca Book Publishers gratefully acknowledges the support for its publishing
programs provided by the following agencies: the Government of Canada
through the Book Publishing Industry Development Program (BPIDP), the
Canada Council for the Arts, and the British Columbia Arts Council.

Cover design: John van der Woude
Cover photography: Getty Images

Orca Book Publishers   Orca Book Publishers
Box 5626, Stn B.   PO Box 468
Victoria, BC Canada   Custer, WA USA
V8R 6S4   98240-0468

Printed and bound in Canada

08 07 06 05 • 5 4 3 2 1

For Lana, Maggie and Matt,
a terrific home team.

Acknowledgements

The author would like to thank the following people:

Publisher Bob Tyrrell for believing in this project
and agreeing to take a chance on it; and editor
Andrew Wooldridge, for his skill and patience
in helping a rookie through his first fiction effort.

chapter one

Matthew Hill cut hard toward the basket, well aware that the taller boy defending him was lunging to keep up. But just two steps into his move, Matt planted his high-top sneakers firmly on the asphalt, quickly reversed direction to the wing and waited for the pass.

There it was, a perfect delivery from his buddy, Jake Piancato. Matt gathered the basketball, and in one smooth motion, leapt and fired it toward the hoop from a dozen feet out. Swish. It was the game-winner and it was a thing of beauty.

"All right!" Jake shouted, rushing over to deliver a high five. "That's four games in a row. We rule tonight, dude."

The sweet sweat of a late-August evening was trickling from Matt's wavy, brown hair, soaking his

T-shirt and making the tips of his long fingers the slightest bit slippery, but he couldn't imagine anything feeling better. Matt and his friends had just won four consecutive three-on-three games on the popular asphalt court of Anderson Park. In these games, you stayed on as long as you kept winning and the line of challengers at the side of the court was growing steadily.

"Who's next?" asked Phil Wong, his voice booming out in mock bravado as he smiled at Matt and Jake. "Who else are we going to have to send home tonight?"

A tall, dark-haired boy with hard eyes who had been casually bouncing a basketball with his friends on the side of the court stepped forward. He was older and more muscular than Matt and his crew. The two boys standing directly behind him were even bigger. "We got next," the lead boy said firmly, a confident smirk creasing his angular face.

Matt recognized him instantly. It was Grant Jackson, the starting point guard on the South Side Middle School basketball team. He had never met Jackson, but he had seen him play plenty of times. Jackson was a terrific ball handler, shooter and defender and he was tough. He had been all-city the previous winter as an eighth-grader and he still had one more season of middle school ball to play at South Side.

This would be a difficult match-up, but Matt was thrilled to get the opportunity. He and his friends would be entering grade seven at South Side in less than a week and they had never played against guys this good. Matt was pumped, but he tried to appear cool. "Hey," he nodded casually at Jackson. "You play for the Stingers, right?"

Jackson ignored him, instead roughly batting the basketball out of Matt's hands near the top of the key. "We'll take first ball," he growled. "You guys aren't going to touch it again tonight."

Matt was a little startled at the hostility, but he settled into his defensive crouch, waiting for Jackson to begin the game. It really should have been Matt and his team's possession to start, since they had won the previous game, but that didn't seem worth making a big deal about.

The Anderson Park rules were simple and rarely varied no matter who was playing. Half-court games were to eleven points by ones and the format was "make-it-take-it," which meant the team that scored got to keep the ball until they were stopped by the opposition.

Even though Matt and his friends were younger than their opponents, they had been playing at Anderson Park all summer, and they had been following a rigorous workout schedule provided by South Side Stingers' Coach Stephens when he had visited

Glenview Elementary back in the spring. This pickup game against actual returning Stinger players – grade nines no less – would provide a good indication of just how much Matt and his friends had improved.

Although the older boys were bigger and stronger, Matt's team was already warm, in rhythm and held a much hotter shooting hand. After an intense fifteen minutes, they were deadlocked at nine points apiece.

That's when Grant Jackson decided to take matters into his own hands. He dribbled the ball from the top of the circle, faked right and then quickly cut left, leaving Matt a half-step behind. Matt reached his left hand out toward Jackson in an attempt to distract his shot, but it was too late. The older boy had already gone up for a jumper, which he efficiently drained. "That's ten to nine," Jackson said. "This one is for the game."

As he took the ball again from the top of the key, Jackson confidently attempted the same move, certain he could score again. But this time Matt was ready. He flicked out his right hand, deflected the older boy's dribble and pounced on the loose basketball. Matt dribbled quickly out over the three-point line and fired a pass back to Phil, open in the left-hand corner. Phil wasted little time releasing the shot. It was pure, tying the game at ten to ten.

Grant Jackson's teammates seemed perturbed. Andrew McTavish, a tall thin boy with an acne-scarred face, had been wide open on the play but completely ignored by Jackson. "Come on, man," McTavish complained. "Take a look!"

Jackson ignored the criticism. Instead, he jumped out aggressively to play defense, shoulder-bumping Matt before he had begun to dribble. Even though he was surprised by the sudden contact, Matt sensed that Jackson was too close to properly guard him. Instinctively, he drove around Jackson and headed for an open lay-up. Matt banked the ball in neatly off the wooden backboard for the winning bucket, and Jake and Phil immediately rushed over to slap hands. It was just a pickup game, but they had beaten actual South Side varsity players. This was huge.

"Nice, man," Phil grinned at Matt. "That was so sweet!"

"It was also a travel," Grant Jackson shot back. "Our ball."

Matt was stunned. His move had been fine, not even remotely close to traveling. But now Jackson was saying it didn't count. This was ridiculous.

Jackson had already picked up the ball, and dribbled it back to the outside. Without checking to see whether Matt was ready, he fired up a perimeter shot. The ball bounced once on the front of the hoop before dropping through. "That's game," Jackson said, flashing his annoyingly cocky grin. "See you boys later."

Another group of players had already gathered at the edge of the court, waiting to take on the winners. "Let's go," Jackson was calling impatiently to them. "You guys are up; let's get started. Our ball."

Uncomfortable, Matt, Jake and Phil looked at one another, silently wondering what they should do. Jackson had clearly cheated. But none of them made a move as the three new players began to take their warm-up shots.

"That's brutal," Phil finally said, looking at Matt. "We won that game. He was just mad you showed him up."

Matt knew his friend was right. He also knew he had to say something. The next game on the court was just about to get started when he cleared his throat and raised his voice.

"Jackson," Matt said, trying to sound as calm as possible. "That was bogus. You guys should be off. We won that game. That was no travel."

The dark-haired boy spun around, his hard eyes narrowing as he walked slowly toward Matt. "That might not get called in elementary school," he hissed. "But it was a travel."

Matt found himself feeling embarrassed, angry and confused all at the same time. But by now, Jackson's friends were falling in behind, ready to back him up, and the new team was calling for the next game to begin. Matt realized there was no winning this situation.

Besides, he had to be home soon, anyway. "Whatever, man," he said to Jackson, "but you know that was wrong."

"The only thing wrong was you three dreaming you could actually beat us," Jackson said derisively. "Why don't you and your little buddies go back to Glenview where you belong?"

The older boys all laughed as they turned and began the next game. Matt, Jake and Phil just grabbed their gear from the grassy patch beside the court and started walking home, remaining silent for the first half-block. Jake finally broke the ice. "What a jerk," he said.

"No doubt," Phil agreed. "I hope that's not a sign of what the kids in middle school are going to be like."

Matt nodded. They were all a little leery about making the transition from Glenview Elementary, where in grade six they had been the oldest kids, to the much larger, slightly intimidating South Side Middle School, where they would be newcomers. Classes were starting in less than a week, basketball practice not long after that, and this incident with Jackson and his buddies wouldn't make their transition any easier.

"Who would want to play with a kid like that?" the blond, curly-haired Jake Piancato wondered aloud. "It's amazing he can stay on any team."

"He's all-city," Matt replied. "But you're right. He's got a problem."

As the boys made their way down Anderson Crescent, the huge maples that bordered the park still showed the green of summer. But light yellow patches had begun to form on a few of the leaves, hinting basketball season wasn't all that far off. Talk soon swung away from the problems with Grant Jackson and back to what had been the summer's main topic—making the South Side team.

"Those guys weren't so good," Jake said. "I mean, we held our own out there, right?"

"We did okay," nodded Matt. "But they weren't really warmed up. Then again, we didn't have Amar here, either."

Matt was referring to Amar Sunir, the trio's other close friend who had been away on vacation with his family for the entire month of August. Of the four Glenview Elementary buddies, Matt thought Amar had the best shot at making the South Side squad.

Amar was a little on the skinny side, but he was almost six feet tall and he seemed to be stretching upward by the day. He was already wearing size ten-and-a-half sneakers, his vertical leap was nearly thirty inches, and Matt even wondered if he wasn't already shaving too.

Amar, whose parents were botany professors at the university, was also a hard working player who had matched Phil and Matt step for step throughout July before he and his family left on a month-long trip to India to visit relatives.

While Matt had a superior jump shot and was a better ball handler, Amar was more athletic and could already touch the ten-foot-high rims in the middle school gym, his mop of unruly black hair flopping wildly every time he leapt. As the coaches always said, height and athletic ability were two things they couldn't teach. You either had them or you didn't. Amar had them both, and Matt was certain his friend would be a lock to make the team, even after not touching a basketball for half the summer.

However, he couldn't say the same for himself, Jake or Phil. None of them were very big. Matt stood about five-foot-seven. He was reasonably quick and athletic and had become an excellent ball handler and steady shooter, especially over an entire summer of practice, but he wasn't tall and he was pretty skinny compared to the older middle school kids like Jackson.

It was worse for Phil, who was only about five-foot-four and built like a fire hydrant. Phil was a hard worker, a dependable athlete, and already one of the best three-point shooters in the city, especially when he got his feet set. But the size factor was definitely going against him too.

Jake Piancato was a different story. He was nearly as tall as Amar, and he was perhaps the purest
athlete of the four. But Jake didn't take basketball
as seriously as the other three. In fact, he didn't
seem to take anything seriously. He had been like
that ever since bumping into Matt in the Lego center at preschool. No matter what happened, Jake
always seemed to take everything in stride.

"You guys think too much," Jake grinned, as
Matt and Phil seriously debated, for the hundredth
time that summer, the odds of them all making the
South Side varsity.

"Better than not thinking at all," Matt shot back.
Phil laughed as Jake playfully smacked Matt across
the back of the head with his gym bag.

The three boys were already at the top of Matt's
driveway. He felt a slight tinge of sadness as he
waved goodbye to his friends. This had likely been
the final pickup game of the summer. Everybody
was busy on the last long weekend before school
started, shopping for supplies and new clothes and
getting ready for Tuesday morning.

"See you guys later," Matt said as he headed
down the driveway toward the dark blue two-bedroom house he shared with his mom. "See you in
middle school."

The three friends exchanged smiles that were
at once slightly nervous and excited. Each of them

knew it was the start of a new era in their lives. School was about to get a whole lot more serious. And so was basketball.

chapter two

Matt peered into the bathroom mirror and carefully examined his chin. He was straining to detect a sign—any sign—of whiskers breaking out, but no such luck. Underneath his pile of wavy brown hair the same smooth baby face stared right back at him.

It was Monday morning, already the start of his third week of middle school and lately Matt had taken to a little more self-examination than usual. Going from Glenview Elementary to South Side had meant a significant social step. Instead of hanging out in the schoolyard with kids as young as kindergarten, the fresh crop of grade sevens he was a part of were now sharing their environment with teens as old as fifteen.

Matt had found it intimidating so far. The grade nine kids seemed so much older in the way they dressed and acted. Some of the boys were already practically able to grow moustaches.

The last couple of weeks had been like a whirlwind, as he and his friends were thrown into South Side Middle School, a sprawling, brown brick campus which was about four times the size of Glenview. With five hundred students, it was nearly triple the population of their old school. Four different elementary schools fed into South Side, meaning Matt was meeting new kids and teachers every day.

School life in general seemed much more grown-up than it had at Glenview. For the first time, Matt and his friends had their own lockers in the grade seven hallway in which they could store their books, lunches, skateboards and MP3 players. Instead of one homeroom teacher who taught them everything, at South Side they had a variety of teachers and moved from one classroom to another for each different subject.

Suddenly, school offered choices too, and even the grade sevens had their own personal class timetables. Matt was excited about the "exploratory" periods available in middle school. It was cool to be able to take woodshop, where students would eventually get a chance to make their own furniture. And although he had been skeptical at first, Matt now had to admit that the cooking classes he had taken so far had already added to the repertoire with which he could surprise his mom.

The excitement of a new school had been tempered by the fact that math was proving even more difficult for Matt than it had been in elementary. And despite the many academic choices offered at South Side, opting out of math was unfortunately not one of them.

Helping to ease the transition to middle school, both academically and socially, was Miss Dawson, the advisory room teacher for Matt and Amar and another twenty-five grade sevens. Each school day began with a twenty-minute session in Miss Dawson's room. It was one of the best parts of the day as far as Matt was concerned. A tall, dark-haired woman with warm hazel eyes, Miss Dawson always seemed to have something interesting to bring up for discussion, and if anyone had questions, she usually had an answer. It seemed like she really cared, which helped Matt feel a little more secure as so many things around him were changing.

Any negatives about the new school were offset by the excitement of sports, in particular basketball. And the excitement had been building for the last two weeks. The team's first tryout practice was that afternoon.

With tryouts came a nervous feeling in the pit of his stomach and a pressure Matt had never felt before. He had put so much hope into making the basketball team at South Side, into following in the footsteps of his older brother, Mark, that he couldn't bear to think about not making it.

He and his friends had spent almost every day of the summer working out. Not just playing basketball, as in past vacations, but actually following the "workout schedule" presented by Coach Stephens when he had visited Glenview as part of the graduating grade six students' middle school orientation program in May. That schedule had included, among other things, two hundred jump shots and one hundred free throws to be practised each day of the summer. It had also included twenty "man-makers" at the end of each workout.

Man-maker was the nickname for a fitness drill that tended to leave most players exhausted and begging for air. It involved a basketball court but no basketball. Players had to run from the baseline, to the near free-throw line, touch that line and then return to the baseline. This was followed by an identical run-and-touch to the centerline, the far free-throw line, and the far baseline. All four trips constituted only one man-maker. And twenty of these at any kind of speed were absolutely draining on a hot summer day.

After two months of this regimen, however, Matt noticed that his body had become firmer and that he seemed to be able to run forever during the evening pickup hoops with the older players in the neighborhood. As the others began to tire in the second or third games, he felt himself getting stronger and faster and was able to push past them on the fast break for the first time ever. The summer shooting practice had improved his range too. He could now consistently hit a pull-up jumper from fifteen feet, and he was making eight of ten free throws on a regular basis. After working on his dribble all summer, he was now almost as good with his left hand as with his right. Matt approached these middle school tryouts knowing he had never been a better basketball player.

Still, was he good enough to make the South Side squad? A voice in his head was telling him not to be so sure. If he had been six feet or taller, like a handful of the boys who would be at tryouts, there wouldn't be any question. But Matt was only five-foot-seven and he was only in the seventh grade. He entered tryouts as one of the shortest players. Would his skills and his fitness level be enough to earn one of the twelve spots on the varsity team? Could he make a big enough impression on Coach Stephens to secure a place even though most of the team would be older?

Matt was well aware that there were good grade seven players coming up from the other schools that

fed into South Side too. Each of them would be going all out for a spot on the varsity. The hard truth
was there just weren't many spots up for grabs.

As he approached the gym, which was tucked into
the west end of the two-story South Side building,
Matt felt the insides of his stomach flipping about
and a light sweat breaking on his forehead. He hadn't
ever been this nervous before. But then again, he had
never had quite as much riding on his performance,
either.

He drew a deep breath as he walked through the
double wooden doors of the South Side gym. The
waiting was over.

chapter three

"Okay, people, listen up," Coach Jim Stephens told the thirty-three players assembled around center court. "I've got three basic rules and if you follow them, we'll be all right.

"The first is that you listen. When I blow the whistle, or I'm talking, you hold the ball and don't say a word. That way, I won't waste my time or yours.

"The second is that you try your hardest all the time. I'm not saying you have to make every shot or get every rebound. We all fail sometimes and we all make mistakes. I can live with mistakes if they come honestly. If I see you're not giving it your best, though, you won't last long here.

"The third rule, and this is the most important one," Coach continued, his voice rising slightly and his eyes narrowing below his bushy gray-flecked brows, "you must respect your coach and your team-mates. There will be no back talking or infighting at South Side. You will be supportive of each other."

As he talked, most of the players listened intently. South Side was the smallest of nine middle schools in the city. But it consistently had one of the best basketball programs, and its constant stream of graduating players was a major reason why the South Side High team was always a regional contender. The biggest reason the middle school feeder program was so successful was Coach Jim Stephens.

A tall, rigid man in his mid-forties who had once been a college basketball star, the no-nonsense coach commanded instant respect from most players. He also had a pretty simple way of operating. If you didn't give him that respect, you didn't last long.

There had been many talented, tall kids who had gone through the school during the fifteen years Coach Stephens had worked there who didn't stay on the team because they couldn't, or wouldn't, follow the rules. There were no exceptions, no matter how good the player. In the coach's world, no one player was ever more important than the team.

"Is all that clear?" the coach said, looking around as heads nodded. "Good then. Let's get started."

Matt surveyed the group, which seemed so much older and more mature than the Glenview Elementary team on which he and his buddies had played for the last three years. He instantly recognized the player directly behind the coach, a muscular boy about five-foot-ten with dark hair and eyes. It was Grant Jackson — the boy from the incident at Anderson Park. But if Jackson recognized Matt, he wasn't letting on.

As Coach Stephens wrapped up his pre-practice talk, Jackson and his friends were smirking at the coach's comments, as if they'd heard this speech too many times before. The boys were laughing quietly about something, but they all went absolutely silent when the granite-jawed coach spun their way.

"McTavish, Jackson, White," he barked at the trio. "Since you guys have been through all this before, why don't you lead everybody in ten man-makers to get us warmed up?"

Jackson's grin disappeared. He raised his eyebrows, but nevertheless hustled down to the baseline to lead the fitness drills. South Side's first practice of the year was officially on.

Once the balls were bouncing and the players moving, Matt's nerves faded into the background. The drills weren't much different than those he had done at Glenview, the players were just bigger and faster. The prospects worked in stations, with a half-dozen players under each basket, concentrating on specific skills such as dribbling, boxing out under the boards and defensive shuffles. For Matt and his friends, just being in the South Side gym with its see-through backboards, glistening oak floor and the huge maroon letters spelling "HOME OF THE STINGERS" painted along each baseline wall, was a thrill. Several times during the session Matt looked around, drew a deep breath and reminded himself to work as hard as he possibly could. He wanted this more than anything.

Near the end of the session, Coach Stephens split the players into groups of four so they could work on both executing and defending the pick-and-roll. Matt had practised this with his buddies all summer, playing two-on-two and developing a keen sense of when to use the pick to get free of his defender and drive hard to the basket, and when to instead fake the shot and drop the pass inside to the post player cutting to the hoop. "If you know how to run the pick-and-roll properly," the coach said matter-of-factly before beginning the drill, "nobody can stop it."

Matt and a beefy grade nine center with blond, spiky hair named Dave Tanner were paired up for this drill. They were matched up against Jackson and his best friend, Andrew McTavish, another of the boys with whom Matt had experienced the run-in at the park just weeks before.

For the most part, Tanner and McTavish played inside while Matt was pitted against Jackson on the perimeter. But near the end of the drill, Jackson nodded to McTavish and the two silently switched places.

Matt followed Jackson into the key as he moved to the free-throw line, posted up and waited for the pass. Matt had a decent defensive position on Jackson as McTavish dumped the ball inside. Jackson caught the pass and spun quickly, cocking his elbow and hitting Matt flush on the jaw. The surprisingly powerful shot rocked Matt backward, bringing the taste of blood mixed with sweat to his mouth and sending him sprawling to the hardwood. Matt was stunned, but he bounced up quickly, wiping the trickle of blood from the side of his mouth with his left hand as he felt his lower lip begin to swell.

One look at the hard-nosed, sneering Grant Jackson standing above him told Matt no apology was forthcoming. Jackson glared down at him with his hard eyes. "Just remember, rook," he hissed quietly. "I'm the starting point guard on this team."

chapter four

Matt stared down at the light brown Cheerios bobbing in the half-full bowl of milk and tried to convince himself that he was hungry. It was 7:00 on the first Monday morning of October, and he wasn't the least bit interested in eating breakfast. Or if he was, his skittish stomach didn't realize it.

His mother was busy making lunches and asking him about school and his friends. But despite sitting just a few feet away at the kitchen table, Matt didn't hear much of what she was saying. His mind was fixed on the list that would appear today. The only thing he could think about was whether or not his name would be on that list.

This afternoon, at 4:00, Coach Stephens would release the names of the twelve players who had made the varsity squad. After two weeks of practice,

Matt wasn't sure where he stood. He thought he had played pretty well, but there were plenty of good kids in tryouts, most of who were taller and older.

Matt wanted to be on the team so badly it was difficult to concentrate on anything else. He had struggled to do his math homework over the weekend, finishing one question and then daydreaming about the team list, then doing another. Even the horror movies he and Jake had rented on Saturday had failed to hold his complete interest. The time between the last practice of tryouts on Friday afternoon and this morning had seemed to stretch forever.

"Matt? Have you heard a word I've said?" his mother interrupted his thoughts, feigning anger. "Maybe if I painted my face orange and wrote Spalding across my forehead, I'd have a better chance with you!"

"Sorry, Mom," Matt replied, forcing a spoonful of now soggy cereal into his mouth. "But today is huge. If I make the team it will be so sweet. But if I don't...I don't know." His voice trailed off. The thought of not making it was too much to bear. There was so much riding on the list.

"If you don't, then you'll make it next year," she said sweetly, laying her small hands on his shoulders and gently stroking his wavy brown hair. "Besides, this isn't the first team you've ever tried out for. It will be okay."

It was true. Matt had been playing organized sports since he first took to the field for mini-mites soccer as a five-year-old. Despite the fact his mom was a single parent, she had always managed to find the registration fees, money for decent equipment and enough time to drive Matt in their chuggy red Toyota Corolla to the baseball diamonds, swimming pools and gymnasiums around the city.

Matt loved sports but none quite as much as basketball, a game he had first seen on television and then later, in a much more real sense, when his older brother Mark was a steady guard on the South Side High School team.

Eight years older, Mark was gone now, working a good job on the oil rigs in Eton, a couple of hundred miles away. Their only contact was on his brother's odd visit home, Sunday-night phone calls and, most frequently, e-mails. But Matt could still vividly remember those winter nights when his mom would make a thermos of hot chocolate, bundle him up in his heavy jacket and mittens and trudge through the snow from their two-bedroom apartment to the high school to watch Mark play.

Back then, when he was only seven and not much more than four-feet tall, high school basketball was a fascinating new discovery for Matt. The cheerleaders giggling and locking arms, the hundreds of people of all shapes and sizes packed tightly into the bleachers, the smell of the sweat and the squeaks of the sneakers on hardwood all mingled into an intoxicating blend. The very first time they visited the South Side High gym, he was hooked on the game.

Ever since then, Matt had spent much of his free time on the outdoor courts of the neighborhood; shooting hoops by himself after school until it got too dark; and playing H-O-R-S-E with his buddies on summer days until they grew tired of laughing at each other's miserable attempts to make the "ultimate" shot. To Matt, there was nothing better than the feeling of a ball in his hand and a backboard in front of him on a sunny afternoon.

And there was nothing more important right now in his life than making the South Side Middle School roster.

Matt's mom noticed the serious look and his furrowed brow. "Come on," she coaxed. "Basketball isn't everything, you know."

Matt had to smile. Somehow, his mom always seemed to have a way of making him feel better, of calming his nerves. And even though she sometimes came out with some pretty weird things—like calling Kobe Bryant "Bryant Kobe" in front of Phil and Jake one day last summer—she still understood him better than anybody else in the world.

Matt and his mother were about as close as a parent and a child could be. His father had left when

Matt was just three, and although he had often wondered what it would be like to have a dad around,
he honestly couldn't think of many times he had felt
shortchanged because of it.

Mom had always been there, even in the early days
when she was a waitress and he and Mark ate supper
in the back booth at the Elmhurst Diner while she
worked. She had saved her tips, always made sure
they had decent clothes and good food and that they
did lots of interesting things like trips to the zoo and
to the park. Even now, when Matt was twelve and
old enough to do most things for himself, she made
a point of taking him out for a pizza or a movie or
to play mini-golf every once in a while. They had
their fights and issues, but more often than not they
enjoyed each other's company.

Matt liked to refer to his auburn-haired mom as
"short but sweet." He liked almost everything about
her as a parent, but he desperately hoped he had inherited his height from his dad, whom Matt understood
was about six-foot-four. His mom stood only five-foot-
two, but Matt loved her big brown eyes, small nose
and easy smile, all traits that he shared. And his mom
had a warm, gentle manner that had helped make him
feel safe and loved as he grew up. He felt he could talk
to her about anything—or almost anything.

Matt had always been able to sense his mom didn't
enjoy discussing his father. It wasn't that she wouldn't

answer questions about his dad, but Matt thought he
could detect hurt in her eyes whenever the subject
came up. For the most part, he simply avoided the
topic. He had gleaned enough to know that his father
was tall, had a mechanical engineering degree, knew
a lot about music and airplanes and had been a pretty
good athlete in his high school days. Matt also knew
his father hadn't been around while he was growing
up. He hadn't seen his dad or had any contact with
him since his parents split up, which meant that Matt
had no real memories of his father. But a few years
ago he had decided that he didn't really need to ask a
bunch of questions if it meant upsetting his mom.

When he was about seven and Mark was fifteen,
their mother began studying for her real estate license,
thinking that if she was good with people in the res-
taurant she might be able to use the same skills to sell
houses. When Matt was nine, she officially became
a real estate agent and, within months, was making
more money. The job change meant they could move
out of their apartment and into a two-bedroom house
about six blocks from South Side Middle School. It
had also meant that Matt had to become more inde-
pendent, making his own meals sometimes and doing
the laundry for his mom after Mark moved out. You
could never tell when Mom's pager would beep and
she'd be called away to show a property or write
up an offer. But no matter how busy she got, she

had always been able to get him to his baseball, basketball or soccer games. And she always seemed to have time to make him feel better when he was worried.

"Basketball might not be everything," Matt said, as he grabbed his backpack and headed for the door. "But it sure feels like it this morning."

"Good luck," smiled his mom, rising to her toes to kiss him on the forehead. "And try to forget about it until this afternoon, okay?"

As he hurried down Anderson Crescent, Matt went over the pool of players and tried to determine which twelve players Coach Stephens would select. Some were obvious, such as Jackson and McTavish and even Amar, who had been impressive during tryouts. But others were on the bubble. Matt couldn't help but feel he was one of those.

His pace quickened as he saw Jake and Phil up ahead, waiting as they always had since elementary school, under the massive oak on the corner of Anderson Crescent and Seventh. Jake lived about five miles outside town at Long Lake, where his parents ran a small resort. Each morning, he took the bus into town, getting off on Densmore Street near Wong's Grocery, the corner store run by Phil's family. Jake and Phil then walked a couple of blocks to Anderson and Seventh and waited there for Matt.

The three of them—four, counting Amar, who walked to school from the opposite direction—had been inseparable since their days at Glenview Elementary, playing sports together, exchanging trading cards and video games and just hanging out. Matt felt comfortable with these guys. He knew they'd remain friends no matter whose names appeared on the team list this afternoon.

"The Mattster," Jake shouted in an overly dramatic television announcer's voice. "What's up?"

"Not much," Matt replied. "Just thinking about the cuts, you know?"

Just seeing Jake put Matt at ease. Of all his buddies, Jake was the most easy-going, and it was difficult not to feel comfortable around him. He never seemed to take anything too seriously, including himself. He was a natural at everything—sports, school, music—without even trying.

"Don't sweat it," Jake said, reaching out and pulling Matt's ballcap down over his eyes. "You worry way too much."

Matt couldn't help thinking that if Jake worried even just a little he'd be a sure thing to make varsity. Jake was about two inches taller and stronger than Matt, but his basketball skills weren't nearly as polished. While Matt and Phil had practised diligently during the summer, Jake had taken it far less seriously. He had spent more time at the beach, watching videos and playing the fire-engine red electric guitar he had taken up in the fifth grade. Jake lived in the moment and, for him, not every moment included working on his crossover dribble.

Matt knew that Jake, who had one of those long-limbed bodies capable of moving quickly and powerfully with almost no effort, had the raw ability to make the South Side basketball team. He was often the best player when the four buddies battled through their summer games of twenty-one and two-on-two. But Matt also knew that for Jake, whose whole family enjoyed water-skiing and hiking and horseback riding, basketball was just one thing, not the only thing.

"I couldn't sleep last night thinking about it," Phil interjected. "I'd be happy just making the team to sit on the bench."

Phil was deadly serious about basketball, or anything else he tried. He was a straight-A student and a competitive chess player and the best video-gamer Matt had ever seen. And he had consistently been the top catcher all through Little League baseball, easily his favorite sport.

Phil's parents ran a popular electronics business downtown while his grandmother took care of Wong's Grocery, the family's neighborhood corner store. Phil was expected to help out at the store in the mornings before school and more often during the summer months. Consequently, he and Matt had spent many a summer day hanging out at Wong's Grocery, helping Phil's grandmother organize the returned soda bottles, stock shelves and sweep up the aisles. The boys had also sampled a fair amount of the candy and potato chip inventory at Wong's and had spent countless summer nights playing Strat-o-Matic baseball and PlayStation2 in his grandmother's cramped living quarters at the back of the store.

Matt believed that Phil worked even harder at sports than he did. But Phil was at least three inches shorter and that would hurt his chances of making the South Side varsity against the larger grade eights and nines. Still, Matt had long ago learned never to count Phil out of anything. Nobody was more persistent. And he had a great three-point shot. He had become something of a folk hero in outdoor pickup games at Anderson Park during the past summer due to his uncanny long-range accuracy. Whenever Phil drained a three, either Jake, Matt or Amar—or sometimes all three—would yell: "Phil it up! Phil it up!" It had become his trademark.

As the three friends walked down the leaf-strewn sidewalk of Seventh Avenue toward the South Side school grounds, Matt couldn't help thinking that each of them was probably on the bubble to make the team. It was good to have their company, especially this morning.

chapter five

The school day dragged on for Matt. He kept staring at the clock, through history, language arts and career preparation in the morning. He half-heartedly played some pickup hoops outside during lunch period, barely picked at the ham-and-lettuce sandwich his mom had packed for him and then struggled mightily to concentrate through his afternoon math class with Mr. Davis.

Math was Matt's least favorite subject and the only one with which he had any real trouble. Mostly, he was a solid-B student, and school had come fairly easily all through elementary. But math, particularly now, was a different story. He just wasn't interested in it because he wasn't much good at it. It seemed to Matt that he had to work twice as hard at multiplying fractions as Phil did, even though his friend always got far superior grades.

Mr. Davis was a portly man, in his mid-forties, with a graying beard and thick black-rimmed glasses. He wore white dress shirts that always seemed to be coming untucked from the back of his pants and his hair was a tangled mess. Matt didn't care so much about that stuff, but whenever Mr. Davis began delivering a lesson he found himself tuning out. With the school year little more than a month old, Matt knew he was already falling behind.

Not being able to follow something that most of the other kids seemed to routinely grasp bothered Matt, but on this day, that concern took a definite back seat to basketball team selections. Finally, after what had seemed the longest fifty-five-minute math period of his life, the bell rang at 3:35. School was out. It was time for the list.

Matt crossed his fingers secretly as he left his desk and kept them crossed as he grabbed his backpack and his basketball gear. He was actually trembling slightly and feeling a little dizzy as he made his way down one flight of stairs and through the after-school clamor of the hallway. He was so focused he hardly heard Phil and Jake as they shouted for him. And he banged into Amar in the hallway as they both sprinted the last few feet toward the gym door. "I hope we all make it," Matt said as Amar nodded silently.

There was already a crowd gathered by the gym where the list was posted so they had to wait until it subsided. Matt felt his stomach churning as the group finally parted and he moved toward the wall where a single white piece of paper, and his future as a basketball player, hung.

The paper was headed: "South Side Stingers, Varsity Boys' Basketball Team." Under that title were a dozen names, typed out in capital letters. Matt's heart thumped so hard he was sure the other boys straining to see the list could hear it. He looked down the names quickly, almost desperately, "JACKSON, TANNER, McTAVISH, SUNIR"—great, Amar made it! —and then finally, second, from the last: "HILL, MATTHEW."

Matt was elated. All the hard work of the summer had paid off. He was on the varsity! As a grade seven! He had to tell his mom. He had to tell Mark. He had to tell the guys. This was awesome.

Matt took another look at the sheet, just to make sure his name was actually there. Then he spun around to find his friends. But the look on the faces of Jake and Phil sobered him. They hadn't made it. They were crushed. Matt didn't know what to say.

"I'm sorry, guys," he mumbled sheepishly, feeling guilty for being so happy just a second earlier.

"Good for you," said Phil, managing a smile. "And good for Amar too."

"Yeah, that's cool for you guys," added Jake, his voice fading a little at the end.

Suddenly, all the noise at the gym door stopped as Coach Stephens blew his whistle. Everyone listened intently.

"Okay, people," said the coach, his voice a notch gentler than it had been through tryouts. "By now, you've all seen the list. And I have to tell you that cut-down day is the worst day of the year for me because I have to tell a lot of you that you didn't make varsity. That's not fun for me or, obviously, for you.

"What I want to tell those of you young players who didn't make it is this: There will be still plenty of opportunity to play basketball this year on the junior varsity team. So don't stop working hard. Remember, that a guy named Michael Jordan didn't make his school team the first year, either. As I recall, he ended up being a pretty good ball player. So keep working and I'll be keeping an eye on you.

"As for the guys on the list, congratulations. We should have a fine team this year. There is no practice today. We'll just hand out uniforms and practice strip and get down to some serious work tomorrow."

Uniforms. Real uniforms, not just jerseys like in elementary school, but uniforms with stylized lettering and piping along the v-neck and shoulders, just like those worn by the NCAA teams Matt and his buddies watched on Saturday afternoons. Matt had been waiting a long time for this. He was eager to secure his favorite number ten in the rich maroon-and-white colors of the Stingers. And the practice jerseys and shorts coach had mentioned were an added bonus. Suddenly, he felt like a professional athlete. This was a very big deal.

Matt and Amar made their way toward Andrea Thomas, the team manager. She was easily distinguished by the bright red cast that ran from her right thigh down to her ankle. Andrea had been a star soccer player for the South Side girls' team that fall. But in just the second game of the season, she had turned her knee under the weight of a falling teammate. The injury had required surgery and she had taken on the job of the boys' basketball team manager while she recuperated.

The blond, blue-eyed Andrea was dutifully handing out practice gear, home and away uniforms and warm-ups, as well as checking each player's name off a list as he received his allotment. Matt's heart was soaring as the line inched forward. But while waiting for his turn, he looked back and noticed Phil and Jake walking slowly out the gymnasium door. For all the joy he felt over being on the team, it was sad to see two of his best buddies left on the outside.

"Ten's my number too," Andrea said as she handed Matt his gear. "Good choice."

Matt didn't know what to say. He managed a shy grin. "Thanks," he mumbled, staring down at the gym floor as he felt his cheeks growing hot.

Matt made his way home proudly juggling his backpack, gear and uniforms still on their hangers. He could hardly wait to get home and tell his mom. He knew she'd be excited. Matt quietly opened the door and was immediately hit by a wonderful smell coming from the kitchen. He could hear his mom humming to herself. He burst into the room. "Mom!" he said. "Guess what?"

"You made the team! That's terrific!" she said, tears forming in the corners of her eyes. "I'm so proud of you, Matthew. What a great day. Let's see your uniform."

Matt spent the next half-hour telling his mom how many games the Stingers would play, which tournaments they would be in and posing for pictures in his new uniform. Then he told his mom that Jake and Phil hadn't made the team.

"That's too bad, Matt," she said. "I hope they aren't too bummed out about it. Those boys worked hard too."

Matt had been so excited that he'd forgotten to ask his mom about the cake she was baking. It was chocolate chip, his Gran's recipe, and it was his favorite. "What's it for?" he said, looking through the glass door of the oven at the rising, golden form in the pan.

"It's for you, of course," she smiled. "It's an I'm-proud-of-you cake."

Matt groaned at his mom's hokeyness. But inside he was also happy she was making a big deal out of this. "But how did you know that I was going to make the team?"

"Matt," she said, her eyes beaming. "I'm proud of you, whether your name is on a list or not."

Later that night, Matt sent an e-mail to his brother Mark, informing him that he had made varsity. Mark had also played at South Side for Coach Stephens, but he had been a late-bloomer and hadn't made the team until grade eight. It was kind of cool to do something his big brother hadn't.

Matt was busy looking up a map of Africa on the Internet for a geography paper when an Instant Message flashed across his computer screen. It was from Mark. "Another Hill stars for the Stingers," it read. "Way to go, bro!"

He could hardly sleep that night. All he could think about was basketball. It was going to be a great year.

chapter six

"Listen up people," Coach Stephens barked.

The South Side Stingers were huddled around their coach before the opening tip-off against Mandela Middle School. "Winters is out for this one. Hill, I'm going to start you at shooting guard in his place. Are you up for that?"

Matt was stunned. Four games into his first season with the Stingers, he hadn't been expecting this. Until now, he had been a bench player, filling in for Grant Jackson at point guard when the older boy needed a breather. When Pete Winters, the Stingers' starting shooting guard, had hurt his ankle in practice the day before, Matt had just assumed that an older kid would take his spot. A grade seven starting a game for the Stingers was something that rarely happened. But it was happening now.

"Sure, Coach," Matt shot back nervously. "For sure."

"Good then, let's go get a win." Coach Stephens put his right hand into the middle of his team huddle. One by one, the players placed their hands on top of the pile. "One-two-three, Stingers!" they chanted.

Matt's legs felt wobbly as he headed onto the court for the tip-off. He had spent most of the first three games of the season on the bench as South Side had roared out to three straight victories. Matt didn't want to do anything to screw up that streak.

As soon as the ball was tossed into the air by the referee, his nerves disappeared. Dave Tanner won the tip, flicking the ball back to Matt. Matt handed it off to Jackson and then headed downcourt to take his position in the offense. He was happy that he had taken the time to study the playbook. He had a pretty good idea of where every player was supposed to be in each offensive scheme, not just the point guard's responsibilities.

On the first possession, Jackson dribbled to the right side across a high screen set by Tanner. Matt cut hard down the baseline, then emerged on the right wing. He was wide open. Jackson found him with a crisp pass and Matt didn't even think before he reacted. He left his feet, releasing the shot at the peak of his jump and following through with his shooting hand as though he was waving goodbye to the basketball. The ball left his hand, hitting the back iron of the rim and spinning gently through the twine. It was two to zero South Side, and Matt had scored the game's first basket.

That game was the most fun Matt could ever re-member having on a basketball court. He made some mistakes, throwing the ball out of bounds once when he misjudged a cut by Jackson, and overthrowing Tanner on a pass inside, but for the most part he played solidly. He finished with eleven points as South Side pounded Mandela seventy-five to thirty. Matt hadn't even realized that he had hit double figures in scoring for the first time until Andrea ran over, dangling the score sheet. "Nice game, number ten," she smiled.

A few minutes later, Coach Stephens sat down beside Matt in the locker room. "I'm proud of how you stepped up today," he said quietly. "Nice going."

Matt had never felt better. The game and the kind words from the coach and Andrea left him feeling great. He felt like putting his gear back on and start-ing practice right this moment. His team was cel-ebrating a win and a perfect four-victory, no-loss start to the season and, suddenly, Matt was feeling like he was a much bigger part of that.

Until this game, Matt was strictly an understudy to Grant Jackson. Jackson was a jerk, but he was also easily the team's best player and he happened to play point guard, so Matt had barely seen the floor during early-season games. Matt had only about five minutes playing time and didn't score in South Side's season opening forty-nine to thirty-six win over the Central Wildcats. And he had played just two minutes in a tougher fifty-four to forty-six decision over the North Vale Nuggets. During the team's third game, a sixty-five to thirty blowout over the Manning Minutemen, Matt had played ten minutes in the second half and scored two baskets, including a nice jumper from the baseline.

Sitting on the bench hadn't really bothered Matt. After all, he was only in grade seven and he still had a lot to learn. Coach Stephens had emphasized that fact to him during practice drills, pushing him to work harder and challenging him to develop his skills. But it hadn't been easy to watch Jackson start each game and play most of the minutes.

About three inches taller and much more muscular than Matt, Jackson was a terrific, tough player with a couple of years of middle school basketball experience. But he was also cocky and cutting and never seemed to have a good thing to say about anybody, especially when it came to the grade sevens on the South Side team and, especially it seemed, when it came to Matt. The hostility probably stemmed from the incident in the park in the summer.

During practice, Jackson and his buddy Andrew McTavish would smirk at the rookies as they ran through drills, whispering to each other and laughing derisively. Matt and Amar could never tell exactly what the older boys were saying, but it wasn't hard to figure out who they were poking fun at. It had been tough to shake it off and just play basketball and the coach hadn't really seemed to notice that it was going on.

Matt had noticed that a distinct division had developed on the team. Jackson, McTavish and a grade nine center named Steve White, sat in one corner of the locker room and even on one part of the bench, right near the far end. They seemed a lot older than all the others and they bragged loudly about wild parties, drinking and girls. It was difficult for Matt to tell how much, if any, of what they were saying was actually true.

Part of Matt was intrigued by this bunch. They were all tremendous players and athletes and they seemed so confident and, in many ways, so grown-up. They didn't seem very nice, though. Matt wondered if that was part of growing up—becoming a little harder, a little meaner. The thought bothered him.

But not all of the grade nines on the team were like Jackson and his friends. Dave Tanner, the Stingers' starting center, was a solid student, a good listener and a friendly kid. Instead of making fun of Matt and the other grade sevens, Tanner and Pete Winters treated the younger guys like they were an important part of the team and often took the time to give them little tips during practice. Dave Tanner might occasionally get frustrated at Matt or Amar when they made a mistake during a game, but he didn't hold grudges and he seemed to remember that he had been a rookie once too.

Until tonight, Matt had certainly felt like a rookie. This game against Mandela had been something else altogether. He had actually started and played well, and he had scored eleven points. Matt had never felt better.

Amar, who had also played well with eight points and six rebounds, seemed happier for his buddy than for himself. "Way to go, Mattster," he grinned. "You were huge out there."

Matt was just getting ready to head to the showers when he noticed Grant Jackson making his way across the locker room. He looked different. The cocky smile and the swagger weren't quite as apparent. He seemed friendlier all of a sudden. "Nice goin', rook," he said to Matt, then glanced at Amar. "Guess the two of you aren't useless dweebs one hundred percent of the time."

Jackson laughed and so did the players in his corner of the room. Matt didn't know quite how to handle this, but he decided to take it as a backhanded compliment. "Everybody gets lucky sometimes, Jackson," he said.

It took half an hour for Matt to finish showering and getting dressed as he savored the afterglow of his breakout game. By the time he glanced at his watch, he was shocked to see it was nearly 6:00 p.m. His mom would be waiting for him

Matt grabbed his gym bag and headed down the empty hallway toward his locker. He had forgotten his math homework, but luckily he could swing by and pick up what he needed before heading for home. Matt was just rounding the corner toward his locker when he heard voices, ringing loudly through the hallway.

"You had five turnovers," barked a deep voice that Matt didn't recognize. "I don't know why you're so happy after a game like that. Keep giving it up and you're never going to get that scholarship."

"Whatever," came the reply. Matt recognized this voice immediately. It belonged to Grant Jackson. "Why are you always on me about stuff?"

"Somebody's gotta keep you focused," came the reply. "You obviously don't care enough to do it yourself."

The voices grew nearer and Matt almost bumped into the pair as they rounded the corner. It was Jackson, all right, and an older man with the same distinct dark hair and eyes. It must be Jackson's dad.

"Hi," Matt said awkwardly.

The two brushed by him, not even noticing he was there, still arguing as they headed out the double doors of the school.

chapter seven

The hallway was crowded as Matt made his way toward Room 107, where he and Amar had advisory period with Miss Dawson first thing every day.

Amar spotted him first and cut immediately away from the girls he was exchanging math homework with.

"Hey, did you hear about Jackson and White?" he asked Matt. "They got caught shoplifting after the game yesterday. Coach and the principal already decided. They're gone for the Middleton game. Suspended. They would have got longer, I bet, if it hadn't just been chocolate bars and magazines that they took."

Matt was shocked. Jackson and White gone for the Middleton game? That was bad news for the entire South Side team. Jackson was their best player, and the Middleton game was for first place. The Marauders had Tommy Layne, who was supposed to be the best point guard in the entire city, and without Jackson the game would be practically impossible to win.

Then the other side of the equation registered. If Jackson was gone, Matt was probably going to have to take his place as point guard for the big game. It also meant he was going to have to go head-to-head with Tommy Layne, who regularly scrimmaged against high school players during the summers.

Matt wondered how Jackson and White could have been so stupid. Shoplifting? Chocolate bars and magazines? What were they thinking? It seemed a strange thing to be doing, even for Jackson. How could a guy who usually made good decisions on the basketball court make such bad choices off of it?

That afternoon at practice, Coach Stephens confirmed that Jackson and Steve White, the lanky back-up center to Dave Tanner, were suspended for one game and would be on what the coach referred to as "probation" for the rest of the season. Not only that, but Jackson and White would have to apologize to their teammates before they would be allowed back.

"I want each of you guys to know that this is serious," the coach said. "I will not condone stealing or any other dishonest actions by players on this team. I am giving Jackson and White one chance.

If it happens again, they're gone. I don't care how good a player is, he only gets one second chance."

Coach Stephens had the players split into pairs and begin the practice by shooting fifty free throws. He pulled Matt aside. "Hill, you have a tough job ahead of you. You'll have to guard against Middleton's Tommy Layne. And Layne will likely be guarding you. It's a huge assignment for a grade seven. But I wouldn't ask you to do it if I didn't feel you could handle it. What do you think?"

"I feel okay, coach," Matt said, trying to sound as confident as possible. "I mean, I can handle it."

Deep inside he was much less certain.

Matt's nerves eased as practice continued. Something about running through the drills was soothing and reassuring. But as they were taking a mid-practice water break, Matt noticed Coach Stephens and another man talking on the far sidelines across the gym. It was Grant Jackson's dad. Matt couldn't hear what the two men were saying, but the visitor was waving his hands as he spoke. From across the gym, it looked like the two were arguing.

Suddenly Jackson's father turned and stalked out of the gym through an emergency exit. He slammed the steel door behind him and the noise reverberated around the gym.

Puzzled, the players looked at each other and the coach. Coach Stephens blew his whistle, completely ignoring the incident. "Okay, people," he shouted, "give me five man-makers and hit the showers."

Matt's mom came to the Middleton game, just as she had for the previous four that South Side had played. It was good to see her there in her usual spot, four rows up in the bleachers behind the South Side bench. He had noticed the unmistakable joy in her eyes when she had realized he was starting for the Mandela game. He just hoped she would be as proud of him after this one as well.

As Matt took his final warm-up shot then headed to the sidelines, he looked up at her. She smiled broadly and yelled, "Go Mats!"

This was embarrassing. His mom hadn't called him that for awhile. "Mats" was a family nickname he'd had since the first grade when, for awhile, he began signing his name in after-school care as "Mats" because he was such a big a fan of the Toronto Maple Leafs' captain, Mats Sundin. His ears burned at the sound of it now and he hoped none of his teammates had heard. But for a minute at least, the thought took his mind off Middleton and off Tommy Layne.

A few seconds later, however, Matt was lining up for the tip-off and sizing up Layne. The grade nine guard was about two inches taller than he was, with a blond brush cut, a lean build, long legs and huge hands. Matt had seen Layne play during the summer at Anderson Park and knew he could do it all — handle, defend, shoot and pass. This would not be an easy assignment.

Middleton controlled the tip and the ball went to Layne. Matt immediately jumped up to defend him tightly, and Layne dribbled the ball upcourt slowly, sizing up his opponent for the day. As he crossed the three-point line, Layne head-faked, shot out his right foot, head-faked again and got Matt to bite. In a blur, he reversed his dribble and drove left down the lane all the way to the basket for a twisting lay-up. It was that simple.

"You're too tight on him, Matt," yelled Coach Stephens from the bench. "Give him some space."

As the game wore on, Matt learned how to better play Layne by not crowding him so much. He managed to keep the senior guard outside most of the time, but in doing so he gave up several open jump shots. Layne was definitely holding the upper hand, but Matt wasn't being completely dominated, either.

Meanwhile, the taller South Side team was stronger in just about every other department. Heading into the final thirty seconds of the game, the score was tied at forty-two to forty-two. The Stingers had the ball and Coach Stephens called a time-out to set up a play for their final possession.

"Okay, people, listen up. Matt, you bring the ball down, and I want you to take some time off the clock.

Wait for Amar to set a screen down low for Tanner. When Tanner comes high, get it to him. Then he can either drive or shoot with enough time left for a rebound if we don't score. Okay?"

Matt nodded. The Stingers broke their huddle. Matt took the inbounds pass from Pete Winters and dribbled upcourt. Layne picked him up tightly, but Matt passed the ball off to Winters. After getting the ball back at the top of the three-point circle, Matt looked at the game clock— there were just ten seconds remaining. It was time to go.

He waited for Tanner to come high off Amar's screen. But as that was happening, Matt noticed that Layne had suddenly started overplaying him well to the right and was completely out of position. Instinctively, Matt began to put the ball on the floor to drive left, through the large hole in Layne's defense. But almost as soon as the ball left his hands, Matt realized he had been tricked. Layne had been playing sitting duck, giving him the space and just waiting for the move. The Middleton guard stuck out his right hand, deftly scooping the ball away from Matt and into his own grasp before heading upcourt.

Layne was all alone on the break, so quick that Matt couldn't possibly catch him. He laid the ball softly against the backboard just before the final buzzer sounded. Middleton had won forty-four to forty-two and Matt's man had scored the decisive basket. Matt was responsible for the loss, and he felt like heading straight out the gym door and home.

On the bench, the Middleton players exploded, surrounding Layne and slapping him on the back. South Side's contingent began to solemnly pick up their warm-ups and head toward the locker room. Matt wished he could crawl right under the hardwood floor. He had screwed up. Why hadn't he just run the play the way coach wanted?

He was sitting next to Amar in the near-silent locker room when the coach approached him. Matt thought he was in for a lecture, but Coach Stephens sat down beside him. "Matt, there's no shame in somebody like Layne getting the best of you once in a while. He's all-city and you're in seventh grade. Don't sweat it too much. These things happen sometimes. It's all part of the learning process."

Then the coach stood, cleared his throat and addressed the entire Stingers team. "Okay, people, let's keep this in perspective. It's one loss and it's the middle of the season. This game could have gone either way. You worked hard out there. Let's not hang our heads. Let's get back to practice Monday and work a little bit harder."

chapter eight

Grant Jackson stood by the blackboard near the coach's office in the South Side gym, looking uncharacteristically uncomfortable. There was no smirk on his face and his dark eyes were darting nervously, trying to keep from looking at his teammates seated on the floor.

"Grant has something to say to you guys," Coach Stephens announced. "Grant, you can go ahead now."

"Um, I'm sorry," Jackson mumbled before moving quickly to take a seat with the other players.

"Hold on," Coach Stephens interjected. "That's not good enough, Grant. Try again."

Jackson reluctantly rose and stood in front of his teammates again. He cleared his throat. "Sorry for letting you guys down," he said. "It was stupid to take that stuff from the store. It won't happen again."

Although Matt thought that even the second apology was less than heartfelt, this one was good enough for the coach. Grant Jackson was back on the team.

With Grant back in the line-up, Matt's playing time dramatically decreased. The Stingers reeled off three more wins to finish the first half of the season at seven wins and one loss. All in all, though, Matt was happy with the way things were going for him and for Amar, who had played his way into the starting small forward position and become one of the team's most important players. Matt was now getting back-up time as both point and shooting guard and rarely played less than ten minutes a game. Amar, meanwhile, was getting even more playing time because of the absence of Steve White, the back-up center who had been suspended along with Jackson for shoplifting. While Jackson had apologized in front of the entire team, White had flatly refused to do so. Coach Stephens' rules were simple and non-negotiable. White was gone for good.

The atmosphere in the Stingers' locker room had subsequently become more united. Jackson's corner crew numbered one less and he and McTavish had begun to talk to the younger players, even joke around with them a bit. The team was still clearly split along the same lines, but it was inching closer together as the season wore on.

The Christmas break seemed to help build team spirit as Coach Stephens held a party for the players and their parents at his house, and the team exchanged gag gifts. Matt got a broken doorknob from Dave Tanner, wrapped up in bright red paper, with a card that read: "Better work on your handle over the holidays."

Matt had to laugh. He was the one player on the South Side squad who worked on his ballhandling every day—almost to the point of obsession. The guys on the team knew that and, Matt thought, they probably respected him because of it.

Matt nearly didn't recognize Andrea Thomas, who had come to the party wearing a black dress, makeup and her hair gathered up off her shoulders. She and her mother made their way over to Matt during the evening. "Mom, this is the other number ten," Andrea said.

"Pleased to meet you, Matt," Mrs. Thomas said. "Andrea's told me about you."

"Nice to meet you too," Matt said, stammering slightly. He suddenly felt embarrassed. "She's a really good trainer for us."

Inside, Matt cringed. What a dumb thing to say. There were a few seconds of awkward silence as he smiled at Andrea and her mother. "I think I'll go get some more food now," he finally said, slipping away from them.

Matt was quiet as he and his mom left the party that night. "What's wrong, Matt?" she asked. "You seem a little down."

"No, Mom," he said. "Just tired."

Truth was, Matt was wondering what Andrea's mother had meant when she said she had heard a lot about him. Like what? He had barely talked to Andrea all season. Matt felt confused yet strangely pleased at the same time.

Matt and his mom spent a quiet Christmas Day together. Mark was working almost non-stop at Eton through the holidays in order to pick up premium shift money, so he couldn't make it home.

When it came time to open their presents, Matt was eager to see his mother's reaction. He had worked for three straight weeks in woodshop making a spice rack for the kitchen, which he had carefully stained in matching colors. She beamed as she opened it.

"This is terrific," she said, reaching out to hug Matt. "I can't believe you made this yourself. It looks like it's right out of a custom kitchen store. Thank you!"

Matt had already opened several gifts, getting some CDs he wanted, plenty of clothes for school and even a white Jason Kidd Nets' home jersey from his brother. There were no gifts left under the tree, but his mother reached behind her chair and pulled out a rectangular present wrapped in green and red paper with a large white bow. "This is for you, Mats," she smiled.

Matt unwrapped the gift. It felt like a box with shoes in it. And it was. But these were no ordinary shoes. His mom had bought him a pair of black Air Jordans with white trim. They were the latest model, just like the shoes a lot of NBA players wore. This was unbelievable. "I thought you might like those," she grinned.

Matt spent the rest of the Christmas holidays hanging out with Jake, Amar and Phil. Strangely enough, they were all looking forward to the return of school and, most importantly, the resumption of basketball. Unlike other coaches, Coach Stephens didn't believe in his team playing or practising over Christmas. "You boys can work out on your own, but the holidays are time for a break—for me and my family too," he had told the team.

It wasn't long before the Stingers were back into the grind of three practices a week. One Thursday afternoon in early January, after practice had finished, Grant Jackson walked over and sat beside Matt's locker room stall. "Hey, Hill," he said, so quietly that Amar couldn't hear. "A bunch of us are going to hang out after the game tomorrow night. You wanna come with us?"

Even though Jackson had been a little friendlier as

the season wore on, Matt was surprised at the invitation. He also realized that Jackson wasn't inviting Amar. It put Matt in an awkward position.

"Uh, yeah, sure," Matt replied, not knowing what else to say.

"Cool, bring your bike. We'll go from here after the game."

As he trudged home that night through the light snow, Matt's mind raced at the invitation. He wondered what sorts of things Jackson and his buddies did for fun. He wondered why, all of a sudden, he was considered cool enough to hang out with them. He also wondered why Amar wasn't, and he felt guilty about that. But Jackson's invitation also felt good, like a sign Matt was becoming part of the "in" crowd. He felt himself looking forward both to the game and to the next evening.

On Friday morning, Matt's mom told him she'd be at the game, sitting in her usual spot. "Do you want to catch a movie afterward?" she asked.

Matt remembered Jackson's invitation. "Not tonight, Mom. I mean, I appreciate it and everything and normally a movie would be great. But some guys from the team asked me to hang out after the game. So I thought I would. Okay?"

"That's okay with me. Sure. We can see a movie any time. But who are these guys? Is Amar going too?"

"No, Mom. It's just some other guys from the team, some older guys. I guess the guy who asked me was Grant Jackson. You know who he is, right?"

"Isn't Jackson the boy who got suspended?" his mom asked. "I don't really know him. And what exactly are you guys going to be doing?"

"Mom. He's just a guy. He's okay. I mean, he's on the team, right? We're just going to hang out with some of his friends. It's no big deal," Matt said impatiently.

"Okay, just remember to call if you need a ride and be sure to make it home by ten-thirty," she said. "And wave to me at the game."

The Jensen Jokers didn't provide much of an opponent that evening for South Side. Jackson was on fire for the entire game, scoring thirty-one points, and the Stingers cruised to an easy seventy to forty-two victory. Matt had ten points in about fifteen minutes of playing time, which was becoming an average game for him as the season progressed.

After his shower, Matt got dressed and noticed Amar waiting for him near the door. "You want to rent some videos tonight? I think my mom is making pizza," his friend said.

"I can't," Matt said sheepishly. "I've got something to do." Matt didn't mention Jackson and McTavish and the rest of that crew. Amar hadn't been invited and, obviously, Jackson hadn't wanted him to know about it. For a second, Matt was torn. He felt guilty for excluding Amar and not telling him about being invited to hang out with the other guys. But Amar made it easier when he turned quickly and said, "Okay, Matt. Later."

Jackson, McTavish, Steve White and a couple of other kids Matt had seen before but didn't really know were outside the locker room door when he emerged. "We've got our bikes here, have you got yours?" Jackson asked.

Matt nodded. By the time the half-dozen boys headed out of the school parking lot, Matt hadn't even asked where they were going. There was a wet snow falling that made cycling down the darkened, slick streets a little tricky. The heavy snow, back-lit against the orange glow of the streetlights, made it difficult to see where they were headed.

They stopped at the end of Densmore Street, about eight blocks from the school. Matt knew it well because Wong's Grocery was at the far end of the block. "Oh, yeah," smiled Jackson, turning on his bike seat toward Matt and the others. "We're loaded up for some revenge tonight. You in, Hill?"

Jackson grabbed at the bag one of the boys—a skinny grade nine named Nate Griffin—was carrying, pulling out several cans of spray paint. It was obvious now that they planned to do some tagging.

Matt had never done anything like this before, but it didn't seem overly harmful. Anyway, he didn't want to come across as a wuss. He could go along for the ride, couldn't he? He wouldn't have to actually spray anything.

"Sure," he said, quietly. "I'm in."

"Good," Jackson said. "Let's go then."

They sped down a slushy back alley behind Densmore on their bikes. It had grown even darker, and Matt wondered again where they were going. He was a few feet behind the others when he noticed they had all stopped behind a large, dark metal garbage container at the back of one of the buildings.

"I'm first," said Jackson, eagerly holding up a couple of the spray cans.

The others watched from behind the trash bin as Jackson gingerly made his way through the snow to the back of a building. He began to paint. A large, crude red swastika took shape across the white back wall. Suddenly, none of this felt right to Matt. He began to get an uneasy sensation in his stomach. He wished more than anything that he was at Amar's, eating pizza and watching movies.

But Jackson wasn't done. He grabbed another can, this one yellow. He started to write something across the back of the building in huge, three-foot-high letters.

As Matt strained to read it in the dark, he started to feel nauseous. Jackson had written "Go home Chinks" in ugly lettering across the wall and had also drawn a crude face with slanted eyes. And what was worse, in one sudden, utterly horrible realization, Matt now knew exactly where they were. At first he hadn't recognized the building because they had come down the darkened back alley. But now he knew: This was the back wall of Wong's Grocery. This was Phil's store. And the kids he was with were attacking Phil's family, maybe not physically but with these horrible words and symbols.

"That'll show them for narcing on me," seethed Jackson, his dark eyes flashing anger.

Suddenly it all made sickening sense to Matt. Jackson and his buddies were targeting Wong's for a reason. This must have been the store where Jackson and White had been caught shoplifting. Phil's grandmother was constantly chasing groups of kids out of her cluttered store because she suspected they were stealing from her. It didn't surprise Matt that she had pressed charges after catching them. But why hadn't Phil told him about this? Matt would have never agreed to hang out with Jackson and his buddies if he had known that they might target Phil's family.

Matt was incredibly ashamed. Phil's grandmother had fed Matt handfuls of candy, bowls of noodles and bottles of Coke and had always let the boys watch TV or play video games in the tiny room at the back of the store. She had always smiled kindly at him and often called him "lucky boy." He wasn't sure if she had meant he was some sort of lucky charm or if he himself was fortunate, but Matt had recognized it for what it was, a term of endearment.

Matt felt almost physically ill. He wanted to get away from this place, from these guys. But he was one of them. He felt strangely paralyzed with fear and shame, hiding behind the dark, cold metal of the Dumpster. A light flashed on in the back room of the store where Phil's grandmother slept. The rickety back door swung open and Matt could see her round face peering out, cautiously. "Who out there?" she called. "Go away now, I call police."

They bolted for their bikes and pedaled hard through the slush to the end of the alley and around the corner to Anderson Park. They stopped with their front tires in a circle. Jackson and his friends were laughing loudly and Griffin lit a cigarette. "Did you check out that old bag?" Jackson sneered, stooping over and putting on a mock Chinese accent. "Oooh, I call police."

Matt wasn't laughing. In fact, he felt like throwing up. He was so ashamed he could barely breathe. But he knew he couldn't show the others how he felt. "I gotta go guys," he said curtly. "My curfew is ten-thirty."

"See ya, Hill," Jackson said. "Yeah, see ya around, dude," smiled White.

The five were still laughing in the park as Matt rode out of sight. He couldn't pedal fast enough as his stomach heaved and a shameful tear trickled down his cheek. He pumped his legs furiously as his bike tires skidded through the wet snow. It was dangerous riding so fast in these conditions, but he didn't care. Anything to put distance between him and the ugliness he had just been a part of.

His mother was asleep by the time Matt arrived home, so he quietly made himself a peanut butter sandwich before heading to bed. But even the comfort food didn't make his stomach feel any better, and there was nothing he could do to ease his conscience.

Sleep didn't come easily that night. Matt was restless in bed, thinking about what Jackson had done and feeling like he had been a part of it too. Part of him wanted to wake his mother and tell her what had happened, just to get the awful secret off his chest. But another part of him didn't want to tell her anything. He was too ashamed and afraid of what she would think. Although his mom was sleeping in the bedroom just next door, as Matt finally drifted off, he had never felt more alone.

chapter nine

The next morning, Amar came to the door, holding his beat-up outdoor basketball in his right hand. "Want to go shoot some?" he asked.

Matt nodded, pulling on the old Nike high-tops that he used for playground hoops. Maybe hitting a few jumpers would make him feel a little better about himself.

"You missed some great pizza last night," Amar said. "I took on all my uncles in PS-2 NBA and I dominated. Where did you have to go, anyway?"

Matt swallowed hard. "My Mom wanted me to do some stuff around the house," he said, hating to lie to Amar. "I wish I could have come over."

The last part was no lie. If he had been at Amar's place last night, hanging out with his friend's uncles and eating pizza, he wouldn't have had anything to do with the incident at Phil's store.

Although it had snowed the night before, the sun had already dried up the streets nicely as the two boys walked toward Anderson Park. It was January, but one of those winter days when playing basketball outside was still possible as long as you kept moving. A long, brown-paneled station wagon pulled up slowly beside the duo and Jake Piancato hopped out the back door. His parents were in town from the lake to get some groceries and supplies as they had plenty of business from hunters at this time of year. So Jake had some time to play ball too.

The three buddies had just begun playing H-O-R-S-E out on the asphalt court where they had practically grown up, when Phil arrived. "Let's get some twos going before we freeze to death," smiled Jake.

Phil nodded and the game began. But it wasn't much of a game. Jake and Matt absolutely crushed Phil and Amar even though Amar was by far the tallest, and likely the best, player of the four. Phil had no energy, no jump, this morning. And his shot was badly off. Normally a frenzied whirlwind on the court, he just didn't seem into it. "What's up with you?" asked Jake.

Phil's face grew serious and his eyebrows furrowed below his close-cropped hair. "Aw, last night some kids tagged our store," he said. "My grandma's pretty freaked out. She doesn't want to stay in the store on her own anymore. And I don't blame her. The stuff they wrote on the wall was pretty bad."

Matt felt a large lump in his throat. He began to sweat and he suddenly felt sick again. Playing basketball, he had almost forgotten about last night. Now it all came rushing back and it felt even worse because he could see that Phil and his family had been hurt.

Phil said that he had to go keep his grandmother company in the store for the afternoon. Jake and Amar talked briefly about the graffiti, shaking their heads. "Wonder who would do that kind of crap?" Amar said to nobody in particular.

It was the worst weekend of Matt's life. Nothing could get his mind off the graffiti and the store or keep him from thinking about how he and his supposed friends had hurt the Wongs. Nothing could ease the shame he felt.

He had to do something. But what? What could possibly make this right? And how could he explain why he was hanging out with those guys? Why had he gone along with them in the first place? How could he explain it to his mother? He needed to talk to somebody about it, but who? He couldn't think of a single person he would dare tell.

The ringing of the telephone interrupted his thoughts. It was Mark, making his usual Sunday call from Eton, a conversation which often involved asking for a loan until payday or for his mom's chili recipe. She talked with him for a half hour, catching up on the latest news and girls in Mark's life. Usually, Matt loved to close his eyes and just listen to the sound of her voice when she was talking to his older brother on the phone. She seemed so happy, so proud. But today even that wasn't enough to make him feel better.

"Matt, come here and talk to your brother for a minute," his mom called from the downstairs hallway

"I can't now," Matt stammered. "I'm in the middle of something."

The truth was, Matt didn't feel like talking to anybody. He could only think about the mess he was in.

Then a thought came to him. Mark! Maybe he could talk to his brother about this. Mark was older, he hadn't always been an angel growing up. Maybe he'd know how to handle it.

"Wait, Mom, I'll take the phone," he called, running downstairs.

After making small talk for a few minutes, Matt stepped into the kitchen, just out of his mother's hearing. "I need to ask you something," he said to Mark. "But I'll send you an e-mail, okay?"

"Sure, Mats," his brother said.

That night, Matt wrote to his brother, explaining the situation and how he felt. He hoped Mark would have an idea on how to handle this. He pressed "send" and the e-mail disappeared. There, he had told somebody. There was no turning back now. All he could do was wait.

After supper, while his mom was out showing a house to clients, Matt signed onto the computer. In his e-mail in-box, there was already a return message from Mark.

It read: "Hey Matt, you're right. You have to do something about this. You have to tell the Wongs who did the graffiti. They deserve at least that much. You have to tell Mom too. She might be mad, but she'll support you. Believe me, I've done worse. If you don't tell anyone, this will be tough to live with. Let me know how it goes. Good luck, Mark."

As Matt read the e-mail, he realized his brother was right. Telling the Wongs was the right thing to do. No matter what the cost.

Matt had to wait until Monday night for the chance to hop on his bike and make his way the eight blocks through the biting wind from his house to Wong's Grocery. It had bothered him all day at school. During basketball practice he couldn't concentrate properly and could barely bring himself to look at Jackson and McTavish.

As he rested the front tire of his bike in the store's black iron rack, Matt felt panicky. How was he going to do this? How was he going to tell his friend what he had done? How could the Wongs possibly understand?

Phil had seen him ride up. "Hey, Matt," he smiled, opening the store's front door with the familiar 7-Up logo on the wide, white handle. "What's up? You want to stay for dinner? Grandma made lots of noodles."

"I'm not really hungry," Matt said, casting his eyes downward as he stepped through the front door and into the dim glow of the tiny corner store. "I just need to talk to you."

Matt and Phil made their way down the center aisle filled with bright cereal boxes, cans of soup and bags of potato chips until they reached a pair of stools near the curtain that marked the entrance to Phil's grandmother's living quarters. They had sat on these stools for hours at a time, discussing major league baseball, Phil's primary passion, and eating penny candy. The memories now seemed so far away.

Phil's grandmother was at the front counter, selling a customer a lottery ticket, and well out of earshot. This was the time, Matt thought. "Phil, I don't know how to say this," he started.

"What is it, man?" his friend replied, a concerned look crossing his broad face.

From there, it all spilled out. Matt told Phil about hanging out with Jackson, White and McTavish and about the spray paint and about how he didn't know what building the guys were going to hit until it was too late. He told Phil how sick the racist graffiti had made him feel, how ashamed he was, and how he hoped they could still be friends.

When he had finished, Phil was silent for a few seconds, staring down at the floor and gathering his thoughts. "Don't worry," he said quietly. "We'll always be friends. As long as you aren't hanging around with Jackson and those other idiots anymore, that is."

Matt felt a rush of relief. Just getting the secret off his chest made him feel alive again. But he knew he wasn't finished. "I want to tell your grandmother, Phil," he said solemnly. "I feel really bad that she was so scared by this."

"Let me talk to her," Phil said. "She doesn't speak English that well, so it could get mixed up if you do it. Don't worry, I'll go talk to her now."

Matt watched, feeling helpless as Phil walked to the counter toward his grandma, a stooped and wrinkled woman in her late-sixties who seemed to be always dressed in a long colorful skirt, a sweatshirt and white tennis shoes. "Grandma," Phil began, followed by a blur of Mandarin words. Even after years of hanging around in the store, Matt couldn't begin to follow their language. He could only judge the conversation by the looks on their faces.

Phil's grandmother glanced slowly in Matt's direction and then back to her grandson. There was no mistaking the hurt in her round, heavily lined face as she turned and walked slowly toward the back room. Phil motioned for Matt to come to the front of the store. "Grandma is going to bed now," he said. "You better go."

Matt passed by Phil's grandmother in the aisle as he walked to the front of the store. She didn't look at him as she headed through the red curtain.

"Phil, I'm sorry...," Matt began, waving to his friend. There was nothing else to say.

The next morning, Matt rose at 5:45, went directly to the basement and grabbed a can of white exterior paint and a brush that had been there since he had coated the fence the previous summer. He hung the paint can over his handlebars as he pedaled his way into a brisk headwind toward Wong's Grocery.

He felt a little better after talking to Phil the night before, but as he reached the back of the store, the shame returned. The Wongs had scrubbed off most of the graffiti, but you could still clearly make out the outline of the horrible messages scrawled by Jackson and his friends.

There was no snow this morning, but it was cold and windy as Matt opened the can and slowly began to paint over the wall. He erased any trace of the graffiti, so it was as though the ugly incident had never happened. But Matt knew better.

The back door of the store opened and Phil's grandmother stuck out her head. She glanced at the paint can, then at Matt and the freshly painted wall. When she realized what he had done, she flashed the warm smile and sparkly eyes that he had seen so many times before. "You lucky boy," she said and she ducked back inside.

Matt returned home just in time to catch his mom at the kitchen table eating a bagel and reading the *Post*. "Where did you get off to so early this morning?" she asked.

Matt gulped. This was it, he thought, his chance to tell his mother. And once he began, the story again poured out of him. He didn't stop, or even attempt to read his mother's soft brown eyes, until he had finished.

She cleared her throat and looked directly at him. "Well, Matt, I have to admit I'm disappointed you would agree to go along with boys who were planning to do something like that. That is somebody's property, and you should know better. But I am proud of the way you've tried to make it right. Please, just promise me you won't hang out with those guys anymore."

Matt nodded. He had absolutely no plans to do that.

chapter ten

For the first time since the graffiti incident, Matt's mind was finally clear, and he was looking forward to basketball practice the next afternoon. But when Coach Stephens blew his whistle to start the session at precisely 3:55 p.m., two players were missing.

"I have an announcement to make," said the coach, speaking slowly and clearly. "And I'm going to make this simple.

"Grant Jackson is no longer part of this basketball team. He was suspended earlier this year for a game and then given one second chance. Last week, as some of you might have heard by now, he did some tagging with Andrew McTavish—a really stupid, senseless, hurtful thing to do. As you know, I only give my players one second chance. Jackson is now off the squad.

"And that's not all," the coach continued. "McTavish has been suspended for one game for his part in it. He will be allowed back after the Churchill game and he, too, will get one second chance."

Matt couldn't believe his ears. Jackson had been punished and so had McTavish. Phil's grandmother must have gone to the principal. But she must have kept quiet about Matt being there that night too. All this came as a shock. Matt had been so overwhelmed with personal guilt since Friday night he hadn't even thought about the implications for the basketball team.

There were more surprises. Coach Stephens informed the team that he was elevating Jake and Phil from the junior varsity to fill the vacancies created by the permanent loss of Jackson and White and the temporary absence of McTavish. Matt's two buddies were going to join him on the Stingers. Normally, he would have been ecstatic to hear this news, but something new was now gnawing on his conscience.

Coach wasn't finished yet. "Hill, you're now the starting point guard," he said. "I know you can handle it."

At that moment, Matt didn't feel like he could handle much of anything. He was still a part of the team, even though he had also been a part of the tagging. As practice continued, he increasingly felt as though he was lying all over again. The final whistle of the afternoon couldn't come soon enough for him.

Grant Jackson was waiting for Matt outside the gym door after practice. His arms were folded across his chest and he wore a bitter sneer.

"Narc," he growled, nearly spitting in Matt's face. "If you hadn't opened your stupid mouth, we'd all still be on the team. But maybe getting your little buddies on the squad was the plan all along."

Matt flushed with anger. "It wasn't my idea to tag that store, to write that stuff. It was yours."

Jackson moved in front of Matt to block his path. He began to raise his arm and Matt tensed, preparing for the blow. But before it was even launched, the door opened and out of the gym strode Coach Stephens.

"Jackson, what are you doing here?" he barked. "Go on home. You're not to hang around here. Do you understand?"

Jackson didn't answer the coach. He just turned away and began walking, but not before casting a menacing glance back at Matt. "We're not finished, Hill."

Coach Stephens looked at Matt quizzically, a wrinkle coming to his forehead as his eyes narrowed and his jaw clenched firm. "What's this all about, Matt? Why is Jackson in your face?"

Matt was speechless. He wanted so badly to just spill the truth to Coach Stephens and get it all out in the open. But he just couldn't bear to have the coach think badly of him. Not when things were going so well on the basketball court.

"I don't know," Matt said quickly. "The guy's just got a problem, I guess."

All the way home, Matt felt lower and lower. Not only had he escaped punishment, but now he had just lied to the coach too. By the time he arrived home, his mom had already come and gone, leaving him a note: "Matt, I have two showings tonight. I'll call you between them. You can heat up the chicken and rice that's in the fridge for dinner. Love, Mom."

Matt was almost relieved that she wasn't home. It would have been impossible to talk to her about school or friends or the house deal she was hoping to close. He didn't feel like talking to anybody.

After finishing his English homework, Matt headed to his room. He flipped the headphones for his MP3 player over his ears and tried to use the pounding of the music to get his mind off his dilemma. But it didn't work.

Whenever he had a problem like this, he went over the problem thoroughly and then over the possible solutions just as carefully. Then he weighed those solutions and chose one.

This time, there were only two choices. Either keep quiet and keep playing basketball, or go to the coach and admit that he had been part of the tagging at Wong's Grocery. That would surely mean some sort of punishment, and he could say goodbye to the starter's job. But the more Matt thought about it, the more he knew it was the only thing to do.

When he woke up the next morning, Matt decided that he would head straight for the school gym and see if Coach Stephens was there. He skipped breakfast, left a note for his mom, who was still sleeping, and jumped on his bike.

Coach Stephens was in his office, going over some Phys. Ed. class attendance sheets when Matt arrived. He looked up and smiled. "Getting some early shooting in today, Matt? That's great. The gym's free."

"No, Coach," Matt replied. "Actually, I need to talk to you."

Moments later, the coach had heard the whole story. "I'm glad you came to me with this, Matt," he said. "That was a good decision. It doesn't make up for what you did, but it's a positive sign.

"Unfortunately, I'm going to have to suspend you," the coach continued. "It's only fair that if McTavish has to sit out a game, you do too. You will be reinstated after the Churchill game. And like McTavish, this is your second chance—the only one you will get with me."

"Okay, Coach," Matt nodded. "I understand."

As Matt walked out of the office, it felt as though a thousand-pound load had been lifted from his chest. It hurt that he wouldn't get to play against Churchill, but he wasn't hiding a dark secret anymore. And besides, Amar, Jake and Phil would all be suiting up. It would be great to see those guys play varsity together.

Matt didn't see Jackson and McTavish waiting by the boys' washroom as he made his way down the hall after his first class of the morning. But by the time he did spot them it was too late. Jackson crossed the hallway and stood in Matt's path while McTavish circled behind him. There were no teachers in sight.

"Hill, you're a major kiss-ass," Jackson said, his dark eyes brimming with bitterness. "Must be nice to be the coach's boy, seeing as you get to play tomorrow and we don't."

"I'm not playing, either," Matt shot back. "I'm suspended for one game, just like McTavish."

Jackson looked surprised. "Who turned you in? Your little Chinese buddy or his wrinkly grandma?" McTavish laughed in the background.

"I went to Coach myself," Matt said. "I told him I was there with you guys on Friday too."

Both boys looked surprised. McTavish had a strange expression on his face, but Jackson simply appeared furious.

"Then you're even a bigger loser than I thought you were," Jackson said, shooting out his right arm and shoving Matt off balance.

Matt sidestepped the older boy and continued down the hall. He didn't care what Jackson thought of him. At least he would be able to sleep that night.

chapter eleven

It was a case of extremely bad timing. The one game for which Mark was able to make it home from Eton was the game against Churchill. And that was also the game for which Matt had been suspended.

Matt couldn't remember being more disappointed. He had wanted his older brother to see him play so badly, to see how much he had improved since the previous summer. Instead, he had to settle for going to the game with his mom and his brother and watching from the stands as the Stingers took on the visiting Churchill Bulldogs. When South Side emerged from the locker room, Matt waved to Jake, Amar and Phil from his seat beside his mom and Mark. Andrea Thomas glanced his way from her spot on the bench and waved. Matt nodded back at her, hoping his mom hadn't noticed.

Churchill traditionally had a strong team, and this year was no different. They had six wins and three losses heading into the game, while South Side had lost once in nine starts, second only in the middle school league standings to the perfect record of the Middleton Marauders and their star Tommy Layne. Matt felt that the Stingers were a better all-around team than Middleton, despite their loss to the Marauders, but Churchill was a deep, well-rounded squad that was capable of giving even a full-strength South Side lineup trouble.

Without Jackson or Matt in the lineup, it was a long night for South Side. Churchill knew the Stingers were short of ball handlers and employed a full-court press for most of the game. None of the South Side guards, including Phil and Jake, who were seeing their first action with the varsity, could handle the pressure. South Side got off to a shaky start and trailed thirty to fifteen at the half.

Despite being with his brother and mother, Matt wasn't enjoying the game much. He wanted to be out there, and he felt bad for Phil and Jake who hadn't had much practice time before the game and weren't familiar with the varsity playbook. Matt had also wanted so badly to be able to show Mark what he could now do on the basketball court that missing this game was demoralizing.

It seemed to Matt like years since the two brothers had even shot hoops together. Since Mark had moved away to work in Eton, Matt had missed him more than he ever thought he would. They had regular contact by phone and e-mail, but it wasn't the same as being able to go for a walk or play catch at a moment's notice. And for Matt it was different being the "man" of the house now that his brother had moved out.

Matt stole a glance at Mark, sitting next to his mom in the bleachers. He wondered what he'd be doing when he was Mark's age, whether he'd be able to move away from home as his brother had. It all seemed so far away from his life in middle school.

As the white- and blue-clad Churchill dancers sped through their halftime number, kids and parents mingled near the gym floor and the concession table. Looking one section to his right, Matt noticed Grant Jackson and Steve White sitting together with a large group of friends. Andrew McTavish, who was serving a suspension like Matt, wasn't with them this time.

The group of boys were laughing loudly and horsing around in the bleachers, oblivious to the disruption they were causing for the folks sitting near them. As they continued, a couple of families got up and moved further down the stands.

Suddenly, Jackson stood up and glared in Matt's direction. Something looked different about him tonight. It was something in his eyes and the unsteady way he was standing.

"Hey, Hill, who's your date?" Jackson laughed, eyeing Matt's mom. "She's real pretty." His friends beside him snickered.

Matt's ears burned and he flushed with embarrassment. He couldn't let this go, not in front of most of the school. But what should he do?

Before Jackson could sit down, Mark stood up beside Matt and his mother. The sight of Mark's six-foot-three frame, chiseled from long days of work on the oil rigs, was enough to silence Jackson. A few minutes later, he and his crew slid quietly out the gym door.

Matt and his family watched the rest of the game in peace. But there wasn't much to cheer about as South Side fell fifty to thirty-eight to Churchill. Despite a much better second-half performance, the poor start was just too much for the Stingers to overcome. It was so difficult for Matt to watch his teammates struggling out there, knowing there was nothing he could do about it.

Matt's mom had to show a house to clients right after the game, so Mark told her he would drive Matt home. He was staying for the whole weekend, which was nice for Mom. While Matt found himself missing his older brother a lot of the time, he knew it was much worse for her. "Hey, bro, let's go for a pizza," Mark said as they pulled out of the school parking lot in his blue pickup. "I'm buying."

They sat in the back booth at Classico's, the neighborhood pizza place that they had been going to for years. They ordered their old standard—an extra-large double cheese, double pepperoni and onions—and a couple of Cokes. It felt good to be with Mark, who shared the same wavy hair as he and his mother but who had inherited the lanky height and the deep blue eyes of their father. Mark always seemed to have a calm, balanced approach to everything, even if he did bring his laundry home from Eton whenever he visited.

"You guys have a decent team," Mark said, eyeing his little brother across the booth. "Probably a lot better when you're actually playing, though."

Matt was happy for the compliment. He told Mark he was looking forward to the final part of the season. The Stingers had eight wins and two losses and still had a shot at first place over their last six games.

"You've got a bit of a problem with that one kid, though," Mark said. "He was drunk tonight. I walked by those guys on the way to the concession before the game and you could smell it fifteen feet away."

For a second, Matt didn't follow what his brother was saying. Then it clicked. Mark was talking about

Grant Jackson. So that's why Jackson had seemed different tonight, thought Matt. He hadn't had a lot of experience with alcohol—just a brief taste of leftover beers when he did the coat check with the Boy Scouts at a New Year's Eve dance the previous year—and this was the first time somebody at his school had been drunk, at least the first time he'd known about it.

Matt explained the background with Jackson, rehashing the night of the tagging at Phil's store. He told Mark that Jackson had seemed to have it in for him since the incident in Anderson Park last summer.

"You have to keep your eye on that kid," Mark said. "He's trouble. Just make sure that you don't get sucked into fighting with him. He just wants to take as many people down with him as he can. Stay away from him and make sure your real friends are around you most of the time."

Matt thought it sounded like good advice. He didn't plan on being anywhere around Grant Jackson if he could help it.

Matt and Andrew McTavish returned for the Stingers' next game, a rematch with the Central Wildcats, whom they had beaten in their season-opener.

With the two starters back in the lineup, South Side had no problem with the Wildcats even though

Central's crowded, humid gym could at times be a hostile place to play. McTavish scored the game's first basket on an assist from Matt, and South Side never trailed, rolling their way to a fifty-six to forty win.

It marked the first time that Matt, Jake, Phil and Amar had played together in a varsity middle school game, and it was memorable. During garbage time at the end of the second half, Coach Stephens had put the four grade sevens on the floor all at once. And on one fast-break play, the ball had ping-ponged between the friends all the way upcourt before ending in a power lay-up by Amar that was so close to being an actual dunk that it seemed to stun the Central crowd into submission. It felt just like one of those dreamy summer days at Anderson Park.

Without Jackson and White in the lineup, the Stingers had also become a much less star-centered and a much more team-oriented bunch. Their best player now was steady grade nine center Dave Tanner, who was averaging fifteen points and eight rebounds a game and who had proven to be a terrific, even-tempered leader. But everybody else was contributing too, right down to Andrea Thomas, the team manager, who had practically become one of the guys as the season wore on.

South Side rolled off four more wins in a row, to run up a thirteen-and-two record heading into the final game of the regular season, a first-place

showdown with Churchill, this time on the Bulldogs'
home court in the northeast end of the city. Churchill
and South Side had emerged as the top two teams
in the league after Middleton faltered during the second half of the season because of an ankle injury to
Tommy Layne.

Churchill, named after the leader of Great Britain
during World War II, was the oldest middle school in
the city and the Bulldogs were a traditional power-
house. Their gymnasium was nicknamed The Dawg
Pound and was typically jammed. For this showdown
with South Side, people were actually lined up outside
a half hour before tip-off, waiting to get a good seat.
As the Stingers passed the lineup on their way into
the locker room, Matt felt a surge of excitement. This
would be the kind of atmosphere he and his friends
had always dreamed about playing basketball in.

Matt had played well during the season-closing
stretch, averaging twelve points and six assists
and taking good care of the basketball. He felt
ready for the match-up with Churchill, which was
led by center Scott Parkins, a talented six-foot-
four grade nine who was being widely touted as a
future city high school star.

Nobody on the Stingers team could physically
match up with Parkins, who was two inches taller and
twenty pounds heavier than Tanner, the South Side
center. But Tanner was smart, defensively dependable

and, for the most part, able to play Parkins to a stand-still.

South Side managed to play Churchill to a twenty-six to twenty-six deadlock at the half, with ten points from Matt, who was easily beating his man to the basket. But Parkins came alive in the second half, hitting a series of soft hook shots over Tanner to give the Bulldogs a five-point lead with just two minutes left.

Coach Stephens signaled for a time-out, calling the Stingers over to the bench. He then looked down the bench and summoned Phil into the game to re-place Pete Winters, who had been cold from outside. Phil looked a little surprised, but he jumped up, un-buttoned his warm-up pants and rubbed his hands together to warm his fingers.

The coach didn't have much to say. "The big things are defense and rebounding," he said. "If we guard hard and get the boards, the offense will take care of itself. But we have to want the ball." His players nodded.

On the ensuing possession, Matt dribbled across the top of the three-point circle. His check was playing him too tightly, so he juked left and began to drive right where a hole had opened up down the lane. The defender from the right wing slid over to try and stop Matt, leaving Phil wide open behind the three-point line. Matt found his friend with a perfect pass. Phil set himself and then launched the ball. It arced high before swishing through the net. Churchill's lead had been cut to two.

The Bulldogs worked the ball patiently upcourt with only a minute remaining. The fans began chanting, "Bull-Dogs! Bull-Dogs!" until it was almost deafening. They wound down the thirty-second shot clock to about eight and then found Parkins posted at the top of the key with Tanner playing behind him. Parkins made a nice pivot and began to swing around for what looked like an easy three-foot hook shot. But Tanner managed to reach out and stab the ball just enough to knock it out of the Churchill center's grasp.

Matt saw the ball, floating loose in the air as if it were suspended. He didn't hesitate, launching his body toward the ball and wrapping his hands around it as he crashed to the floor, sandwiched between the burly Parkins and another Churchill player.

The referee blew his whistle and signaled it was South Side's ball. Coach Stephens called for his team's final time-out.

Trailing by two points, at fifty to forty-eight, with just thirty seconds left, the coach wanted to go for the safe play. In the huddle, his instructions were simple. "Matt, you handle the ball unless you're doubled," he said. "When the clock is at about ten seconds, get it to Dave. McTavish, you set a screen low for Tanner and free him up. Okay? Let's go."

Matt took the inbounds pass from Phil. He worked it upcourt, slowly, patiently. With thirteen seconds left, McTavish set a textbook screen for Tanner, but Churchill was clearly expecting the play. Two defenders collapsed on the South Side center at the top of the key. The result left McTavish all alone near the baseline.

Matt didn't hesitate. Even though he was open himself, McTavish was more so. He fired a bullet inside that the lanky grade nine forward caught. McTavish spun toward the hoop and laid it in as a flying Parkins crashed into him.

The referee's whistle blew. He was motioning down with his hand. The basket counted, and McTavish would go to the line for a free throw with one second left. Matt stepped forward. At this moment, it didn't matter that the player shooting was Andrew McTavish. He was a Stinger and he was a teammate. "Let's go, Macker. Wrap it up," he grinned.

McTavish smiled back. He stepped to the line. For a second, the steamy gym seemed to freeze. He launched the free throw. It bounced three times gently on the rim before falling through the hoop. South Side had won the game fifty-one to fifty and taken the regular season championship.

chapter twelve

If there was one player capable of spoiling the Stingers' shot at a city championship it was Tommy Layne, the star Middleton guard.

That put the pressure squarely on Matt's shoulders. He would have to guard Layne when they met the Marauders in a city quarterfinal playoff.

Middleton had slipped badly during the final part of the regular season after Layne was sidelined for a half-dozen games with an ankle injury. But the Marauders' star was back now, healthy, and Matt knew he was in for the biggest challenge of his brief basketball career.

It was Layne who had embarrassed Matt by stealing the ball for the game-winning basket earlier in the season. As classes began on the morning of the Friday playoff, Matt just kept thinking about Layne, and how he couldn't afford to make the mistake of playing the Middleton star too tightly.

It was impossible not to dwell on the challenge as Friday wore on. Unlike regular-season games, the South Side student society staged an elaborate pre-game pep rally in the gym during lunch hour. Principal Walker made a speech and so did Coach Stephens. The school's precision drill team performed a few numbers. Then the coach asked Dave Tanner, the Stingers' captain, to step up to the microphone and say a few words.

"It's been a great year," the beefy center with the spiky blond hair grinned awkwardly into the microphone, looking more than a little uncomfortable. "I don't know what else to say. We'll do our best."

Matt felt proud to be a Stinger and excited about the playoffs as he stood there with his teammates. He spied Miss Dawson standing off to one side. She waved and smiled proudly at him, her hazel eyes beaming.

By the time tip-off rolled around, the South Side gym, which sat about four hundred people, was jammed. Matt got a huge boost when he looked for his mom in her usual spot and saw his smiling big brother sitting next to her. Mark had made the drive down from Eton and would finally get to see him play—and in the playoffs too.

The teams lined up for the start of the game and shook hands with each other. Tommy Layne's huge right hand overlapped Matt's, but he smiled and winked at his younger adversary. "Have a good one," Matt said.

The fans who had shown up on what was a bitterly cold, snowy afternoon weren't disappointed. South Side and Middleton played neck and neck throughout the first half and the teams headed into the locker room tied thirty-two to thirty-two. Layne had outplayed Matt, scoring ten points by the half, but he had also had some trouble containing Matt's crossover dribble. The Marauders' star had three personal fouls at the half while Matt had picked up just one.

Coach Stephens was pleased in the locker room at the break. "We're in good shape here," he said. "We're a much deeper team and, as the game wears on, we'll be able to run away on these guys.

"Matt, you're doing a good job on Layne," the coach continued. "In this half, concentrate on taking the ball right at him. I think you can foul him out. You're quick enough and smart enough. If we can get him out of the game, it's over."

Layne began the second half on fire. He made two quick threes to put the Marauders up by six and seemingly in control. But the next trip down the floor, Matt remembered the coach's advice. He shoulder-faked Layne to the right and then put the ball on the floor and cut hard left. As the Middleton guard backpedaled to stop the anticipated drive, Matt pulled up for the jumper. Layne swung his right arm toward Matt but was slightly off balance and bumped his elbow. The shot missed, but Layne was whistled for a foul.

Matt stepped to the line. He was nervous. He had never shot free throws in such a pressure-packed situation or in front of such a big crowd. He missed the first one, as the ball unluckily rolled off the front of the rim and spun out. But he bore down, dribbled the ball twice and swished the second attempt. South Side was within five points now, and Tommy Layne had picked up his fourth foul.

The teams battled hard back and forth, with Middleton clinging to a small lead. With about ten minutes left, Matt found himself with the ball at the top of the key again. He noticed that Layne was overplaying him to the right side, just as he had done in their first meeting of the season. But this time Matt recognized that Layne was again playing coy, trying to set up the steal. He made a move left, but when Layne lunged for the ball Matt quickly crossed over his dribble, cut right and drove for what looked to be an open lay-up. Before Matt could lay in the ball, however, he felt an arm across his back and he lost his balance, crashing to the floor and twisting his right ankle under his own weight.

The pain was horrible as Matt limped to the free-throw line. Then he realized that the foul was on Tommy Layne. The Marauder star was gone.

Matt made both his free throws, pulling South Side to within one point. But his right ankle was throbbing. Coach Stephens sent Jake into the game to replace Matt.

Matt was disappointed about coming out. But Coach Stephens was happy with him. "Nice job on Layne," he said. "Just have a rest. I've got a good feeling about this one."

As Matt sat back on the bench, Andrea hurried over to him with an ice pack and carefully secured it to his right ankle with a roll of cloth bandage. The ice deadened some of the pain, making the ankle feel numb. Matt knew now that he wasn't going back into this game.

But it didn't matter. Without Layne in the line-up, Middleton couldn't stay with the Stingers. Jake turned in his best performance since being promoted to the varsity, scoring twelve points and teaming up with Phil to handle the ball perfectly. And McTavish led all scorers with twenty-five points, including a nice behind-the-back assist from Phil in the game's dying minutes. The final score was South Side sixty, Middleton fifty. The Stingers were going to the city semifinals.

In the locker room, Matt sat in his usual spot with a fresh ice pack on his ankle, which by then already felt considerably less sore. McTavish crossed the locker room, a smile on his face. "Nice job on Layne, man," he said. "Things were a lot easier with him out of the way."

"Thanks," Matt replied. "Twenty-five isn't a bad night for you, either."

It was the first time he had ever really talked to McTavish. And suddenly, he didn't seem like a bad guy at all. As the two spoke, Phil walked out of the showers and looked their way. "Sweet pass, man," McTavish shouted at Phil. "Just like Jason Kidd."

Matt wondered how his friend would react. Phil knew that McTavish had been part of the group that tagged his family's store. He knew that McTavish and Jackson had been close friends. But Phil must have sensed the same difference in McTavish that Matt had noticed. "Way to finish it off," he said to McTavish. "You had a monster game tonight."

Later, Phil asked Jake, Matt and Amar if they wanted to come and hang out at the store for the rest of the night. One of his grandmother's friends was having a seventieth birthday party, and she had asked Phil to look after things for a few hours.

They agreed to meet at the store at eight o'clock. Then Phil shouted across the locker room. "Hey, McTavish, you want to come over too?"

McTavish nodded. "Sure, that'd be cool." He didn't say anything else and neither did Phil. They didn't have to.

That night started off in terrific fashion with the boys watching the 76ers-Bucks game on the portable TV set near the back of the store. Phil brought out some Cokes, chips and a couple of boxes of cookies, and the five boys sat around talking hoops.

It was just about ten and almost time to close up the store when Matt saw them coming down the street. Grant Jackson was walking at the front of a group of kids, including a couple of girls Matt didn't know. He was weaving slightly as he made his way down the sidewalk, headed for the store. Matt cringed at the thought of what was coming.

Jackson came through the door first, looking around with contempt. He didn't even seem to see the other boys, but he noticed Phil behind the counter. "I want some smokes," he demanded aggressively, the smell of alcohol strong enough to detect from across the aisle.

Phil cleared his throat. "You know I can't sell you cigarettes, Jackson," he said calmly. "You're not old enough. My grandma could lose her license if I did that."

"Screw that," Jackson said impatiently. "What are you gonna do if I just decide to take them. You gonna stop me, Wong-Ton Phil?"

Jackson made a lurching move toward the edge of the counter near where the cigarettes were kept. But Phil didn't even have time to respond. Andrew McTavish had already sprung in front of his former friend, halting Jackson's clumsy bid for the cigarettes. A flash of surprise crossed Jackson's face and his dark eyes flickered in disgust. "Oh, so now you're one of the China boys too," he snorted. His friends laughed behind him. But the two girls they were with tried to look the other way, like they wished none of this was happening.

McTavish didn't respond to the taunt. He moved closer to Jackson and stood face to face with him, just in front of Phil near the cash register. McTavish was two inches taller and maybe ten pounds heavier than Jackson. "You should leave, man," he said quietly between clenched teeth. "This isn't cool."

"I'm not going anywhere," Jackson shot back. "What's up with you, anyway?"

McTavish didn't back down, staring straight into Jackson's cold eyes. Jackson's right arm shot forward, shoving McTavish roughly back into the counter, but still McTavish didn't respond. It was clear he was trying to keep his cool, to avoid a fight. All he wanted was for Grant Jackson to turn around and walk out of the store.

But Jackson wasn't about to do that. And as the two boys stared at each other, Matt noticed Nate

Griffin moving from behind Jackson around the right side of McTavish. It happened so quickly that Matt didn't have time to think about how to react. Griffin suddenly rushed McTavish from behind, knocking him in the back of the head with an elbow. Matt saw that Jackson was about to move in on the now stunned McTavish.

Matt stepped forward. Before Jackson realized what was happening, Matt had already thrown the punch. His right fist glanced off Jackson's nose. Matt felt the cartilage slide under his knuckles. Blood began to trickle from Jackson's numb face as he stumbled backward, hardly believing what had just happened.

Matt steeled himself for Jackson's response, but it never came. The older boy backed out of the store, a different look on his face than Matt had ever seen. Jackson's friends followed and so did the girls. In seconds, the store was quiet again. But everything about the night had changed.

"Holy crap!" Phil yelled. "Did you see Jackson's face?" The other boys nodded their approval in Matt's direction.

Matt's head was whirling with a mix of emotions he had never felt. He had never punched anybody before, except in play fighting, and his right knuckles were already swelling up. It had happened so fast that he hadn't had time to think about what he was doing. He was feeling a lot of things, but he wasn't proud at this very moment. Just confused.

Matt glanced up at the clock that hung over the store counter. It was 10:15. He had just enough time to get home on his bike. "I gotta go guys. I have to be home at ten-thirty," Matt mumbled. The others nodded. "Me too," Jake said. "I'll ride part way home with you," McTavish added.

As Matt made his way to the store's front door, Phil caught up to him. "Thanks," he smiled. "That guy is seriously out of control."

Matt managed a weak grin in response and waved goodbye with his left hand as he walked outside. He climbed awkwardly onto his bike and joined the others riding down the street. His right hand was almost too numb to properly grasp the handle bar. It had been a weird night, and he wasn't quite sure how he felt about it yet.

chapter thirteen

By Monday morning, the swelling on Matt's right hand was gone, but the last three knuckles were still bruised and extremely sore to the touch. As he prepared for the walk to South Side Middle School, he had to be careful when pulling his backpack over his shoulder that he didn't catch the strap on his injured hand.

Matt had left the house a few minutes later than usual, so Jake and Phil weren't under the tree waiting for him this morning. They had already headed off to class. He shuffled through the coating of powdery snow that covered the sidewalk, completely alone with his thoughts.

He had been dwelling all weekend on the punch he had thrown at Grant Jackson, going over the scenario that had led up to it and wondering if he could have done anything to avoid it.

Part of him felt good about what he had done, about finally standing up to Jackson and being there to support his buddy, Phil. Andrew McTavish had also seemed surprised and grateful that Matt had stepped in to stop him from being ambushed. Matt played the scene over and over in his head and each time he came to the same conclusion: He'd had no choice but to do what he did.

That didn't make it any easier, though. Matt had never fought anybody—not seriously, anyway—and he had certainly never hurt anybody on purpose. Even though he didn't like Grant Jackson, he couldn't erase from his memory the startled look on the boy's face, and the sudden vulnerability he had seen in those normally cold, dark eyes. That part he wasn't proud of. Not at all.

Neither was he too keen about his mom finding out that he had punched another kid, not even a bully like Jackson. She had always been pretty strict about fighting. She didn't like it at all. Once, in middle school, his older brother Mark had scrapped another boy on the soccer field after school and Mom had grounded him for a week. Matt had so far avoided telling her about the incident with Jackson and had done his best to hide his sore hand from her. But hiding stuff didn't make him feel very good, either.

Matt was almost at the school when he heard Amar's voice from behind him. "Matt, wait up," he yelled, loping across the street, his backpack bouncing off his lean frame.

The two boys walked side by side into the school, headed for Miss Dawson's advisory period.

But before they could get to Room 107, Matt heard another voice behind him—a firmer voice. "Matthew Hill," said Mr. Walker, the principal. "Can I have a word with you for a moment? Not you, Amar. You go on ahead to advisory. This is a private matter."

Amar shrugged and continued on his way. Matt's face flushed with embarrassment. He didn't have a clue what this was about. But getting called into the principal's office first thing Monday morning couldn't be good news. Mr. Walker, a short, stocky man dressed in a blue blazer, striped tie and black pants, was standing beside the door to his office, motioning for Matt to join him inside. Matt gulped hard. There was no avoiding this.

Mr. Walker closed the door behind him and gestured for Matt to take a seat in one of the two brown leather chairs neatly arranged across from his desk. Matt sat down, not feeling the least bit comfortable. This was torture.

"I'm going to get right to the point, Matt," Mr. Walker said, looking straight into his eyes. "I've been told that you were involved in a fight on Friday night. I've also been told that Grant Jackson has a broken nose as a result of you hitting him."

Matt was reeling. How did the principal know about the incident with Jackson? Who had told him? Certainly not Jackson. And a broken nose? Suddenly Matt began to feel nauseous. He didn't know what to say.

"It wasn't really a fight," he mumbled. "I was actually trying to stop a fight."

The principal began to interject, but once Matt had started, the entire story gushed out of him without a break. He told Mr. Walker about Jackson coming to Phil's store and demanding to buy cigarettes, about McTavish stepping in to defend Phil and about how he had then stepped in to help McTavish.

"I didn't mean to hit him," Matt said earnestly. "It just happened. And I didn't even know his nose was broken."

Principal Walker's experienced gray eyes carefully surveyed Matt's face. It was several seconds before he responded. And just as he was about to say something, a knock came at his office door. "Come in," he said.

Through the door walked Coach Stephens, who nodded at Matt. "I asked the coach to join us for this meeting, Matt," Principal Walker said. "It concerns him too."

Matt didn't know what was coming next, but he was pretty sure he wasn't going to like it. Coach Stephens didn't look happy as he folded his long, lean frame into the chair beside Matt.

"I was informed about this incident by Mr. Jackson, Grant's dad," the principal continued. "He was furious that Grant's nose had been broken, and his version of what happened that night is much different than the one you've told me.

"Regardless, fighting is simply not tolerated amongst South Side students. Matt, you haven't been in any real trouble before this and I understand from talking to you and others that you felt you were defending your friend, so I'm going to give you a break. You won't be suspended from school, but I do have to punish you. As I said, fighting isn't tolerated.

"Coach Stephens and I have discussed it and agreed on one week of detention. Now, I'm not going to keep you from basketball practice. I don't think that would be fair to you or to the team. So you'll have to serve the detention in the morning. I expect you to be here at 7:15, in my office, for the next five school days. I'll have some work for you to do each morning."

Matt nodded. He was ashamed but relieved at the same time. It was the first time he had ever received more than a few minutes detention after class, and he wasn't looking forward to getting up early for the next five school days. But at least it wouldn't interfere with basketball.

"You should also know," Principal Walker continued, "that Grant Jackson has been suspended from school for three days. Because he has already been disciplined several times this year, his punishment is far harsher than yours is. But if I see something like this from you again, you'll get similar treatment."

Matt left the principal's office with Coach Stephens and was about to head for advisory when the coach tapped him on the shoulder and motioned toward a bench outside the main office. "Have a seat," he said solemnly.

"You put me in a very tough spot here, Matt," Coach Stephens said. "Normally, two times breaking the rules would mean you were automatically off the team. I had to fight hard for you with Mr. Walker to keep you playing basketball for South Side."

The coach went on to explain to Matt that there would be no third chances. "I know you were defending your friends. But sometimes you just have to make the best decision for yourself. The best decision in that case would have been to get help, not throw a punch," he said. "Your behavior and your decisions have to be exemplary from now on. If something like this happens again, it will be the end of basketball for you this year. Do you understand, Matt?"

Matt nodded glumly and headed toward class. Miss Dawson was already halfway through her topic for the morning. The theme of the day was personal responsibility. As Matt quietly slid into his seat, she was talking about being responsible for your actions and making good decisions, even when you find your-self in a tough situation. Never had advice seemed more appropriate.

Amar leaned across his desk and whispered, "Matt! What's up? What did Walker want?"

"I'll tell you later," Matt whispered back, turning his eyes toward Miss Dawson.

Telling Amar and the rest of his friends would be easy. Telling his mom about this, Matt knew, would be a much different story.

Practice that afternoon was more intense than it had been all season. The Stingers were scheduled to meet the Manning Minutemen in a semifinal that Friday. They had easily beaten the Minutemen twice during the regular season. South Side was a clear favorite to win and advance to the city championship game, but Coach Stephens obviously wasn't taking anything for granted.

"Don't take Manning lightly," the coach said as he opened the practice with a five-minute chalk talk. "Yes, we won pretty handily when we played them, but they had a great game against Eastdowne last week and they deserve to be in the semifinal. Everything that happened in the regular season is history now. It doesn't matter. What matters is showing up ready to play on Friday."

Coach Stephens had the second unit play a one-three-one zone defense for much of the practise session, the same defense that Manning had used with great success during its late-season run to the playoffs. The Minutemen were a young team, with three grade sevens starting, but they were also tall and long-bodied and when they extended their hands on defense, they tipped a lot of passes and made their share of steals. They also controlled the boards.

Matt and his fellow starters—Amar Sunir, Andrew McTavish, Dave Tanner and Pete Winters—worked the ball quickly around the zone during practice. Coach Stephens showed them how to move the ball to one side and then quickly reverse it to the other to find the open shooter. South Side hadn't played against much zone defense all year, but as the Stingers passed the ball, their command of the concept grew. Everybody was looking forward to the semifinal.

"Great practice," Coach Stephens said, as he wrapped up the session. "Three more like that and we should be in good shape for Friday."

Matt glanced up at the gym clock. It was almost 4:45 and practice was over. Normally, he would have been happy to head for home. But today he was dreading it. He would have to talk to his mom about the detention and tell her about the fight.

He grabbed his stuff quickly, skipping his usual shower and heading for the gym door. On the way out, he ran into Andrea, who was collecting the practise balls from the court. "Hey," she said gently. "I heard about the other night. How's the hand?"

"It's okay," Matt replied. "I've gotta go, though. See you around."

By the time he arrived home, Mom's car was already in the driveway. There was no avoiding the situation now and Matt knew it. It was time to face the music.

He opened the front door and headed for the kitchen. But he didn't get past the living room before he heard his mom's voice. "Matthew, can I speak to you?" she said firmly. Any time he heard the full "Matthew" he knew she was serious.

Mom was sitting on the sofa in the living room, looking out the window when Matt entered the room. She patted the cushion and motioned for him to sit down beside her.

"Mom, I have to tell you something," he began.

"I know," she said with a sigh. "I got a call from Principal Walker this morning."

There it was. She already knew. Matt felt a sudden sense of relief. He told his mom what had happened on Friday night, how he felt he had no other choice at the time, how badly he felt about breaking another kid's nose, even if the nose belonged to Grant Jackson.

"Matt, I'm not angry with you for what you did," she said. "It sounds like a very difficult spot to be put in. And I have to admit I'm proud you would stick up for your friend, even if you didn't choose the best way to do it. The best way is always to use words and not your fists.

"What I am disappointed in, though, is that you didn't tell me about it. I want you to tell me these things, Matt. I might have been able to help you sooner."

Looking at it in hindsight, Matt knew his mom was right. He still didn't know what else he could have done with McTavish about to be clobbered, but he knew that it would have felt better, at least, to tell her about what had happened right away. He told her about Jackson's suspension from school and about his own detention.

"That will mean some early mornings for both of us this week," she smiled.

Mom had made pork roast with mashed potatoes and green beans for dinner. Matt poured himself a large glass of milk. As he sat talking with his mom about the upcoming game against Manning and about the houses she was trying to sell this week, it occurred to Matt that food had never tasted better.

chapter fourteen

Six-thirty came way too early, as far as Matt was concerned. The obnoxious beeping of his clock radio stirred him out of a deep sleep, reminding him that it was Tuesday morning and, more to the point, the first of his five early morning detentions.

Principal Walker had made it clear that Matt was to be there precisely at 7:15. Matt wondered why the principal was at school so early himself when classes didn't start until 8:55. He barely had time to scan the *Post's* sports section as he wolfed down a couple of pieces of toast. By the time he grabbed his books and his practice gear, it was already 6:58. He had less than twenty minutes to make it six blocks.

Matt was still breathing hard when he reached Principal Walker's office. But the principal was there, cradling a cup of coffee as he looked over a stack of paperwork on his desk. "Good morning, Matt," he said pleasantly. "Nice to see you're here on time. That's a good start to what I hope will be a productive week for both of us."

"Now, I have been speaking with Miss Dawson about you, Matt," the principal continued. "She feels it would be the best use of our detention time this week if we concentrate solely on math. That seems to be the only academic area where you're having any serious problem."

Great. Not only did he have to be at school at 7:15 for the next five days, but now Matt was going to have to do math for a full hour-and-a-half before regular school even started. The thought of it wasn't appealing in the least.

Mr. Walker cleared his throat before continuing. "As it turns out, Matt, you're in luck. Before I became principal, I was a bit of a math specialist. So, you see, we're a pretty good fit."

Matt managed a weak smile as Principal Walker pulled out a set of math worksheets. "Get started on these and we'll talk in a few minutes," he said. "There's a pencil sharpener in the office lobby if you need it."

Matt looked over the sheets. It was basic multiplication and division. While it wasn't his favorite, at least he understood how to do it. But there were loads of questions and they would take forever to work through.

By the time the first detention session was over,

Matt was already tired and the real school day hadn't even begun. He had four more mornings of this to look forward to. That punch he had thrown at Grant Jackson had been costly, indeed.

As far as Matt was concerned, Friday couldn't come fast enough. He was looking forward to the semifinal against Manning more than any game he had ever played. A win and the Stingers would be in the city finals. Although South Side had made consistent trips to the championship game over the years, Matt and his buddies had never played in a game like this before. This was exciting.

On Wednesday morning, Principal Walker handed Matt another stack of worksheets. This time, they contained math problems that were like brainteasers. Again, these included concepts with which Matt was familiar, but there were more than twenty questions and they were complicated. Just minutes before the regular school day was about to begin, the principal sat down on the front of his desk, facing Matt.

"Good work. Tomorrow, we're going to do something more exciting. I guarantee it," he said with a smile. "I'll see you then."

Exciting? Matt doubted it. If there was one thing math most definitely wasn't, it was exciting.

The next morning, Principal Walker wasn't sitting at his desk when Matt arrived at 7:14. But a couple of minutes later, he strode into his office, carrying a copy of the morning *Post* and some blank sheets of paper. This time he had no worksheets.

"Matt, I know that you're not crazy about math," the principal said. "But I'm pretty sure you like sports, right? And I happen to be a big basketball fan myself."

Matt nodded. He wasn't sure what Principal Walker was getting at.

"Here's what I want you to do today then," the principal continued. "I want you to take these NBA standings from the paper. They show each team's wins and losses. I have cut out the columns that show winning percentage and games behind the lead. That's your job. I want you to figure those numbers out."

Matt's heart soared. This wasn't math, this was basketball. This was more like it. There was just one problem. He didn't know how to do what the principal was asking him to do.

"I'll show you one and then you can do the other twenty-nine teams," the principal said. He then took the Los Angeles Lakers' record of thirty wins and twenty-five losses as an example. The Lakers had played a total of fifty-five games and had won thirty of them. Principal Walker showed Matt how to determine that this amounted to a 54.54 winning percentage. "The NBA lists that at .545," Principal Walker explained.

Matt had never realized exactly what the .545 had ~nt in the NBA standings. But now he did, and not only that, he understood how to figure it out. Next, Principal Walker showed Matt the mathematical formula for determining how many games trailing teams stood behind the leaders in each division.

"The rest is up to you, Matt," he said. "Give me a complete set of standings before school starts."

Matt set out to work. By the time the detention ended, he had a set of standings, complete with a "games-behind" column. He checked it against those listed in the paper and, except for a couple of small mistakes, it matched. It felt good to do something right when it came to math.

On Friday, Principal Walker used National Hockey League goals-against and shooting percentage figures to show Matt how those were computed. By the time his final detention of the week had ended, Matt was almost sad to see it end. Almost.

"Matt, I'm going to give you an early birthday present," Principal Walker said with a smile as the detention ended. "You've worked so hard this week, that you don't have to come back Monday morning for your fifth detention. Just make sure we don't have to have another of these little sessions, okay?"

Matt shook his head in agreement. His birthday wasn't until August, but he wasn't arguing with the principal.

Walking down the hall toward advisory, Matt suddenly had the feeling of a man freed from a jail sentence. Not only was detention over, but so was the wait for the semifinal match-up against Manning.

He and the rest of the Stingers felt ready. Practice had gone well all week. The team was confident it could break the Manning zone defense. There were no major injuries to speak of, only the bruised knuckles on Matt's right hand. But that had bothered him less and less every day this week.

It seemed like the entire school came out to the noon-hour pep rally. Coach Stephens thanked the students for their support and said his team would try its best to earn a spot in the city championship game.

"We're ready," Captain Dave Tanner promised the cheering crowd. "We've been ready for this game since last Friday."

The atmosphere in the locker room was relaxed as the Stingers dressed in their white home uniforms with the maroon piping. Matt slipped on his number ten jersey, wearing a maroon T-shirt underneath as he had all season. He laced up his black and white high-top Air Jordans carefully, making sure, as was his superstition, to tie the left before the right. He grabbed a ball from the wooden bin and dribbled it on the locker room floor as he waited for Coach Stephens to address the team.

"People," the coach began, "you've worked hard all You've worked hard all week. You are ready, and now it's just a matter of continuing to work hard over the next forty minutes. Let's go earn ourselves a spot in the city championships!"

There were more than four hundred people in the packed South Side gym. As the Stingers emerged from the locker room, the crowd erupted in a huge cheer. Matt felt a surge of adrenaline as he took his first lay-up of warm-ups and surveyed the packed bleachers.

Up behind the South Side bench, Matt saw his mom and Mark, just as they had promised. They waved and he waved back. His eyes wandered around the gym, picking out some of his friends and their families and even Miss Dawson in the stands. But he stopped abruptly when his gaze picked out the dark-haired boy with the bandage across his nose sitting under the far basket. It was Grant Jackson.

Matt hadn't seen Jackson since the incident at Phil's store a week earlier because the older boy had been suspended from school. Obviously, he was back. No time to think about that now though. There were more immediate things to deal with than a jerk like Jackson.

The buzzer sounded twice to remind players that there were only two minutes left until the game started. The Stingers headed to their bench. The players circled their coach and put their hands together in a pile of fingers and wrists. "One-two-three," Dave

Tanner yelled, followed by the entire team in unison: "Stingers!"

From the opening tip, Matt knew this game would be different than the two South Side had played against Manning during the regular season. The Minutemen looked like a whole new team as they lined up on the court. They were bigger than the Stingers and they had a newfound confidence in their eyes. South Side was in for a fight.

Tanner lost the tip and the ball went to Manning. Matt tightly defended Travis Green, the grade seven Minutemen point guard, and he seemed to have Green in trouble near the top of the key. But Green simply pivoted, looked inside to six-foot-five post Kenny Forshaw and lobbed the ball up toward the basket. Forshaw leapt above Tanner, caught the ball and flipped in a lazy hook shot for a two to zero lead.

Matt raced the ball downcourt before Manning could properly set up its zone. Green was a step off him and Matt went up for a jumper. Forshaw left Tanner inside and attempted to block Matt's shot. But instead of releasing the ball at the peak of his jump, Matt deftly flicked it inside to Tanner for the open lay-up. It was two to two.

The game see-sawed back and forth, with neither team going more than a half-dozen points up on the other. Manning's height was making it difficult for South Side to work the ball inside consistently, so the

Stingers had to rely on the outside shot and the running game. Meanwhile, South Side's foot speed and quickness allowed the Stingers to "front" the taller Minutemen on defense, denying easy passes inside.

With less than a minute left in the game and the score tied fifty-four to fifty-four, Green again found Forshaw in the middle of the key with a perfect pass. Tanner had good defensive position, but the big Manning center caught the ball, turned and tossed the right-handed hook over Tanner. It bounced softly once on the rim and dropped through. The Minutemen held a two-point lead with just twenty-five seconds left. The crowd packed into the bleachers in the South Side gym, which had been loud and boisterous all game, suddenly went quiet.

"Time-out!" Coach Stephens yelled from the bench. The Stingers hustled across the hardwood to their coach. They huddled around him, hands on knees and eyes fixed on the long, experienced face in the middle.

"Okay, guys," Coach Stephens said calmly. "This is what we practise for. We are in good shape here. This is our last time-out, so I have to set up the rest of the game right now."

Coach Stephens diagramed a pick-and-roll with Matt and Dave Tanner for the next possession. It had been working nicely all game, so Matt was confident it could work again.

"After we score, we need a stop," Coach Stephens continued. "I want you guys to go right into our full-court press. It should catch them by surprise. Nobody can afford to go to sleep here, okay? Once we score—and I just know we're going to score—jump right into that press. Everybody know their position in it? Okay, let's go."

The Stingers broke their huddle. Matt took the inbounds pass from Pete Winters and headed up the court. The clock was ticking down, and Matt waited for Dave Tanner to work himself into position.

Tanner made a quick move to the top of the key, where he stopped to the right of the free-throw line. Matt faked Green left and then dribbled hard to Tanner's right. The pick worked perfectly. Sensing that Matt would shoot, both Green and Forshaw lunged out at him, leaving Dave Tanner alone underneath. Matt found him with a bullet bounce pass. Tanner laid it in softly. The game was tied up with just ten seconds left. Manning called a quick time-out, sending the players back to their benches. All of the Stingers grabbed water bottles and towels to dry the sweat from their arms, hands and faces. Coach Stephens still looked calm. "Listen up," he said. "Our plan is the same. Let's press them right off this time out. Let's get that ball back. But be careful. We don't want any fouls."

The players nodded. They headed back onto the court as the home crowd cheered. This was just the kind of dramatic game that Matt had only ever watched on TV. It all seemed slightly unreal, as if even now he was watching it instead of actually playing in it.

Green took the ball out of bounds from the referee. He looked down the court, but no one was open. Matt could sense Green was beginning to panic, so Matt purposely fell a step off the player he was guarding. Green saw the space and fired the inbounds bounce pass toward Matt's man. But Matt had anticipated the reaction. He shot out his left hand, stabbing at the ball and getting just enough of it to deflect it away from his check. Anticipating Matt's movement, Pete Winters bolted forward and intercepted the ball in the backcourt. Winters saw Matt open near the free-throw line and fired a hard chest pass toward him.

Matt reached out and caught the ball with two hands, just as Forshaw crashed into him, catching his right hand with a hard elbow. The pain seared through Matt's bruised knuckles, but he held onto the ball as he was jolted backward a couple of steps.

The whistle blew. The crowd hushed. Everyone looked toward the referee, who was signaling a foul against Forshaw. South Side was in a double-bonus situation. "Two shots!" the referee yelled.

Matt was stunned. He was going to the line with a chance to win the game, but his right hand hurt worse than anything he could ever remember. The Manning coach used his last time-out, trying to freeze Matt at the free-throw line.

The Stingers headed back to their bench once again. Andrea took an ice pack from her trainer's kit and put it on Matt's right hand. That made it feel a little better, but Matt knew that shooting wasn't going to be easy.

There was nothing for Coach Stephens to say. They simply drank water and rested. Matt knew what he had to do. Nothing the coach said now was going to make any difference. He was still going to be all alone at the free-throw line.

The buzzer sounded. Every one of the South Side players patted Matt on the head or shoulder. "No problem, man," Phil said as he winked at Matt.

Matt's knees were weak, and he felt slightly dizzy as he made his way to the free-throw line. The court had never seemed longer than it did now with hundreds of eyes watching him walk its length from the South Side bench. He had always imagined himself in this kind of situation, but never had he known how it felt until this very moment.

Both teams lined up along the key. The referee was just about to hand the ball to Matt when a familiar voice rung out across the gym. "Hill, you suck!" Nobody seemed to notice where the taunt originated, but Matt had no doubt. It was Grant Jackson, sitting just down the baseline from the basket where Matt was about to shoot the two most important free throws of his life.

Slightly unnerved, Matt took the basketball from the official and bounced it twice, as was his usual routine at the line. Try as he might, he couldn't erase Jackson's taunt from his mind, even though he knew he should be concentrating solely on the rim. He bent his legs and began to go through the shooting motion that he had practiced thousands of times before.

Out of the corner of his eye, Matt saw Principal Walker talking to Grant Jackson, leading him away from his seat. Jackson shook his elbow violently, as if he was literally trying to shake the principal off him, and headed for the door. Nobody else on the floor seemed to notice the drama, but it was impossible for Matt to concentrate while all this was going on.

All these thoughts were whirling through his head as Matt released the free throw. And as soon as it left his fingers, he knew something was wrong. It simply wasn't hard enough and it was badly off line. The ball clanged off the right front edge of the rim and the crowd groaned. Or at least that's the way it seemed to Matt.

"One shot!" the referee shouted, handing the ball back to Matt.

One shot. The Stingers' season had come down to one shot. Matt knew that he couldn't let his teammates down. He drew a deep breath, bounced the ball twice again on the floor and bent his legs. The jam-packed gym had gone completely still.

Matt began his free throw motion. He flicked the ball from his right hand, waving his right wrist goodbye as he released it. This time the ball traveled upward in a perfect arc, coming down through the middle of the twine. It was good. South Side had won the game.

The crowd erupted. The South Side players jumped off the bench and mobbed Matt near the top of the free throw line. Eleven other players were hugging and jumping around him and Coach Stephens was looking at him with a huge grin on his face. Matt glanced up into the stands where his mom and brother beamed proudly. He was pretty sure nothing had ever felt quite this good.

chapter fifteen

Phil whistled as he carefully surveyed the score sheet in the din of the South Side locker room. "Nineteen points, nine assists, no turnovers," he yelled across the room to Matt. "Not bad, bud."

"Nineteen and nine? I had no idea," Matt replied, trying to sound nonchalant but feeling his cheeks glow nonetheless. It had been his finest game of the year and it couldn't have come at a better time. South Side was going to play for the city championship, and Matt was a big reason the team was headed there. Still, being singled out in the locker room, even by Phil, was a little embarrassing.

The Stingers had worked hard all week to prepare for Manning and now, several minutes after the final buzzer, they were kicking loose. The mini stereo system that Dave Tanner kept in his locker room stall was blasting out the tunes while the players laughed and joked and just enjoyed a moment for which they had been aiming all year.

Tanner switched off the music as Coach Stephens walked into the center of the room. The coach was usually all business, but tonight he looked relaxed and satisfied.

"Guys, I want to congratulate you," the coach said, looking slowly around the room. "Manning gave us a tough fight, but you didn't back down. You guys were in a tight spot in the final minute and you showed your character.

"It's great that we won and it's terrific that South Side will get a shot at its twelfth city middle school title. But what I'm really happy with is the way you guys handled yourselves. You made me proud out there and you made your school proud."

The room erupted in cheers. But the coach wasn't quite done. "Just one more thing," he said. "Take the weekend off. But come back ready to work on Monday. We've got North Vale in the city finals here next Friday and if we want to be having a bigger celebration then, it's going to take the same type of dedication I saw from each of you this week.

"Now enjoy yourselves and have a rest. I'll see you at practice Monday."

Matt, Phil, Jake and Amar were the last ones out of the locker room. The win had felt so good that they just wanted to savor it, to make the wonderful mixture of joy, satisfaction and physical exhaustion last as long as possible. Looking at his three closest friends, Matt knew they would be the nucleus of the South Side team for the next couple of years and that was a pretty exciting thought.

It was dark by the time they headed out the front door of the school. Matt had arranged to meet his mom and Mark back home, so they didn't have to wait around at the school for him to shower and change. It would only take him twenty minutes to walk home for what would certainly be a family victory celebration. Matt could hardly wait.

As they made their way up the street, Matt noticed another cluster of boys standing on the corner that marked the edge of the school grounds. One of them was leaning against the chain-link fence with the others gathered around him, talking loudly and smoking. The tallest one, a boy in baggy jeans and a red ball cap, looked up as Matt and his friends approached. He tapped the arm of the boy standing in the middle to get his attention.

Matt saw the bandage on the boy's face and knew instantly who it was. Grant Jackson and his buddies must have been waiting outside ever since he got kicked out of the gym. Matt didn't know why they were still there, but he was pretty sure it wasn't for any good reason.

"Hey, Hill, where are you and your girlfriends go-ing? To Coach's house to suck up some more?" Matt knew the voice as Nate Griffin, one of Jackson's best friends and one of the boys who had tagged Phil's store a few weeks back.

Matt knew he had to ignore the taunt. He quick-ened his pace, hoping that he and his friends could simply walk by without anything happening. He didn't need this kind of trouble now.

None of the five said a word as they moved past Jackson and his group. Matt felt a tiny rush of relief. Maybe they could get out of this, he hoped. But the notion had barely crossed his mind when he felt an icy blast to the back of his head. Jackson had tossed a snowball that had beaned him squarely. The ice crystals stung as they glanced off the bare skin of his neck, but Matt kept walking, his back now to Jackson and his friends.

"Hill, we're not finished," yelled a threatening voice. Matt knew it was Jackson this time. He spun around. "Yes, we are, Grant," he said. "I don't want to fight you. I didn't mean to break your nose in the first place. Let's just forget the whole thing."

It was an apology of sorts, but it seemed only to make Grant Jackson angrier. He rushed toward Matt, pushing him hard off the sidewalk into the snow. The sudden move took Matt by surprise, sending him spill-ing backward and his gym bag flying. Jackson didn't stop, lashing out with his foot, and Matt, now lying on his back, instinctively put up his right hand to deflect the blow. The hard toe of Jackson's boot made contact with Matt's bruised knuckles. The pain was almost unbearable, but Matt tried his best not to wince.

"Get up and fight, Hill, you loser. You're the reason I'm not on the team anymore," Jackson was seething. "Come on. I kicked your butt on the court and I'll do it here too."

Matt felt a surge of anger. It was all he could do to stop from hurling himself headlong into the older boy. But he knew what the cost of that would be. This time, he held back.

Matt turned around, gathered up his gym bag and began to walk away. His friends joined him. "I always knew you were a wimp, Hill," Jackson sneered.

His ears burning, Matt walked faster. In a minute, he and his friends were safely a half-block away from Jackson and his crew. Jake was the first one to speak. "Why did you let him do that to you, Matt?" he asked. "One shot to the nose and Jackson would have been history."

"It's not worth it," Matt replied. "Grant Jackson isn't worth it."

The friends walked on in silence. Matt knew he had done the right thing. If he had gotten up swinging and popped Jackson in the face, it would have probably felt good in the short term, but it would have also meant kissing the city final goodbye. He would have let all his teammates, his family, his coach and himself down. There had been no choice but to walk away. So why didn't he feel better about it?

By the time he arrived home, Matt's right hand was killing him, the outside knuckles swollen up to nearly twice their normal size. The thrill of the big win was gone, replaced now by a feeling that he had let Jackson walk all over him and maybe even ruin his chance for a good game in the city finals. How was he going to shoot and handle the ball with such a sore hand?

Mark met him at the door. "Matt!" he grinned. "Awesome game, man. You were great. Almost as good as a certain former South Side star who went by the name of Hill."

Matt managed a flickering smile in return, but his older brother sensed right away that something was wrong. "What happened to you?" he asked, noticing Matt wince when they shook hands. "It's all bruised and swollen."

The next twenty minutes were spent going over the post-game confrontation with Jackson. Mark and his mom listened intently. When he was finished, his mom spoke. "Matt, I know this is difficult to understand, but what you did tonight was the bravest thing you could have done. It was far braver than fighting that boy.

"You know," she added sweetly. "I was really proud of you on the court tonight. But after hearing that story, I think I'm even prouder of the way you handled yourself afterward."

Mark winked in Matt's direction. "I had a feeling from the start that loser was trouble," he said. "Don't let him get to you, Mats. You were right. He isn't worth it."

They sat down for dinner and a complete play-by-play rehash of the victory. His mom had made lasagna with garlic bread and an apple pie for dessert. Between the company of his family and a terrific meal, the problem of Grant Jackson slowly faded from Matt's mind.

What didn't go away as easily, however, was the swelling in his aching right hand. When Matt woke up on Saturday morning, it was the first thing he felt. He could barely move his last three fingers and it hurt just to touch anything. It seemed worse this morning than it had the night before.

Matt was eating a piece of toast with his left hand when the doorbell rang. Jake Piancato was standing at the front door, his trademark goofy smile creasing his broad face framed by those golden curls. He had a basketball tucked under his left arm and a donut in his right hand. Typical Jake, Matt thought, always ready to enjoy life, one hundred percent.

"Mattster!" said his friend. "Let's go. We can be first for twos if we hurry to the rec center. I'm thinking total gym domination today."

"Sorry," Matt replied. "I'm out for today. My hand is killing me. I can't even eat breakfast properly, let alone shoot hoops. It was sore before, but Jackson got it pretty good with his foot when he kicked me last night."

"That guy is a major jerk," Jake said. "I don't know what his problem is. I know he got booted off the team and I know his dad is pissed, but that stuff isn't your fault."

"I know," Matt said. "Jackson has been like that with me ever since that day in the summer at Anderson."

"He's jealous," Jake shot back. "Maybe because you're a better point guard than he ever was."

Matt smiled despite the pain. Jake was a loyal buddy.

"I was thinking quite a bit about last night," Jake continued, after swallowing a big bite out of his donut. "You were right to walk away from Jackson. I had forgotten that you already had a suspension this year. Coach would have turfed you for fighting. And we can't afford to lose you for Friday. Not against North Vale."

"I just hope I can still play," Matt replied. "This hand is brutal."

The two moved into the living room. Now that playing basketball was out of the question for that day, they plopped down on the sofa and turned on the television. If they couldn't play hoops, they could always watch the NCAA Tournament. It was the first weekend of the sixty-four-team event and most of the teams were still alive. Matt loved watching the way CBS switched back and forth, going from the end of one close game to the next. He couldn't think of anything else on television that he'd rather be watching. Seeing the teams, the cheerleaders and the buzzer-beating shots made him even more excited about playing Friday's big game against the Nuggets. If he was able to play, that is.

chapter sixteen

Matt had never given much thought to what it would be like to be physically disabled. But by Monday morning, he felt as though he had a pretty good idea.

His right hand was still so sore he was unable to grab anything with it, leaving him to get by with his left. Now simple things Matt had never given a second thought to, like getting dressed in the morning or tying his shoes, were either impossible on his own or required considerable planning and effort.

Matt's mom helped him put his backpack on as he headed out the door for school. It felt weird, taking him back to kindergarten and winter days when she used to tie strings to his mittens and attach them to his jacket to make sure he wouldn't lose them at school. At the same time, he was happy to have her there to help him out.

"I want you to get that looked at today," she said, eyeing his hand. "I'll take you to the clinic after practise."

Matt nodded. He knew that unless his hand improved considerably, it would make it impossible for him to play well against North Vale on Friday. He had hoped all weekend that the hand would be a lot better by the time practice resumed, but it was still pretty much useless. And as Matt headed for school that day, he knew he would have to tell Coach Stephens about it right away.

Phil and Jake were waiting in their usual spot under the oak tree as Matt trudged toward them. By this time, e-mails and phone calls had alerted both of them to the status of their friend's injury. Neither said much to Matt, purposely avoiding the topic of his hand and instead chatting about what had happened over the weekend in the NCAA Tournament.

When they arrived at South Side Middle School, Matt turned to his buddies. "Guys, I'll catch you later," he said. "I have to go talk to Coach about something." Phil and Jake nodded. They didn't have to ask. They knew what the subject of that discussion would be.

Matt made his way down the long hallway to the gymnasium. It was empty at this time of the morning because most students didn't get to their lockers until just before the first bell. When he reached the door of the coach's office, Matt knocked lightly. "Come on in," came a voice from inside.

Matt opened the door to find Coach Stephens reading the *Post* and drinking coffee from a large mug emblazoned with the words: *Basketball is life. Everything else is just details.*

"Hey, Matt," the coach said. "All ready for a big week of practice?"

"That's what I came to talk to you about," Matt replied solemnly. "It's my hand."

A look of concern flashed across the coach's face. He listened intently to Matt's recount of what had happened with Jackson. And when the story was finished, Coach Stephens said, "Let me see the hand, Matt."

The coach examined Matt's extended right hand, carefully surveying the knuckles for about thirty seconds. "I can bet it's painful," he said. "You'll need to get that checked out by a doctor to make sure it's not broken."

Matt nodded. "Do you think it'll be better in time for Friday?" he asked hopefully.

"Hard to tell," the coach said. "Let's see what the doctor says. We'll get Andrea to give you plenty of ice during practice. And you should avoid using it or, obviously, banging it against anything during the next few days. We'll have to see by Wednesday how you're doing. But if it's really bad, Matt, I don't want you to try to play. It's a big game, but it's only a game. There will be other big games for you, I'm sure."

Other games? Matt couldn't even think about other games. Friday was the game he had been waiting for all his life and now he might not even be able to play. He couldn't believe Coach Stephens could be so calm about all of this. Matt certainly didn't feel that way.

"Go on to class and try to forget about it," Coach Stephens said as he got up from behind his desk. "We'll see you at 3:55 sharp for practice."

Matt headed down the hallway toward Room 107, his advisory class. Miss Dawson was the only one in the room when he arrived. She was marking her way through a pile of papers but glanced up and smiled when Matt walked into the room. "How's the basketball star this morning?" she said. "Ready for the big game?"

Before Matt knew it, he was telling Miss Dawson all about his injury and the altercation with Grant Jackson and his fears about not being ready for Friday's game. It was weird, but ever since he had started going to South Side that fall, he had sensed that Miss Dawson was somebody he could trust. She asked a lot of questions and she really seemed to listen when he answered and her advisory themes made a lot of good, common sense. Miss Dawson shook her head slowly as she inspected his knuckles. "That looks really sore," she said. "It's too bad, Matt."

By this time, other kids had begun pouring into the room, including Amar and Andrea. Matt took his seat and waited patiently through Principal Walker's announcements.

When they were over, Miss Dawson stood up and moved to the center of the classroom. This was a time when students could discuss things that interested or concerned them and a time when Miss Dawson could impart some of what she liked to refer to as "life's lessons." Mostly, it was a way for her to stay firmly in touch with the group of students for whom she was specifically responsible.

"How's everybody doing this morning?" Miss Dawson asked. "I know, I know, it's Monday, and you'd all just as soon it be Friday…

"The theme for this morning," she continued, walking toward the chalkboard, "is adversity." She picked up a piece of white chalk and spelled the word out across the board, emphasizing each letter with an underscore. "Can anybody tell me what this means?"

Several hands shot up. Miss Dawson spied Amar's arm in the air first and pointed toward him. "It's like something hard or difficult," he said. "You know, like Duke had to overcome adversity against Kentucky to win its game in the NCAA Tournament on Saturday."

Matt had to laugh. Amar had managed to bring basketball into the advisory topic and the session wasn't yet two minutes old.

"Right, Amar," Miss Dawson said. "And do you know something else about adversity?"

This time no hands rose. The room was silent.

"Well," she said, picking up the chalk again. "Adversity can build something. Does anybody know what that something is?"

Again, silence. Miss Dawson began writing. When she finished, the board read: "ABC — Adversity Builds Character."

"Think about anything you have ever accomplished that you have considered, in the end, to be worthwhile," Miss Dawson said. "Didn't most of those things involve overcoming some kind of adversity? If you aced a test, didn't you overcome the adversity of not knowing the information in the first place? And didn't you overcome the adversity of being too tired or too busy to study? Success and satisfaction are almost always the result when you manage to overcome adversity."

Matt looked across the room at Andrea. She was the only one in class dressed in shorts because of the long, red cast that extended from her right thigh down to her ankle. She was watching Miss Dawson intently.

From time to time during the rest of the school day, Matt thought about the topic of that advisory period. His own adversity this week was nothing compared to what Andrea was going through. He didn't have a cast on his hand and he still had a chance to play basketball. But first he had to stop feeling sorry for himself and give himself a fighting chance to work through this injury.

Coach Stephens stood over the circle of players seated in the middle of the South Side gym floor. He looked as serious as Matt could ever remember seeing him.

"Okay guys, listen up," the coach began. "We have four practices to get ourselves ready for North Vale and the city championship game. We've worked hard to get here and we need to keep up that hard work if we want to be successful in our last game of the year."

Coach Stephens gave the Stingers a brief synopsis of the North Vale Nuggets and what they could expect from the opponent that had finished third in the regular-season standings. North Vale wasn't overly big—in fact the Stingers were on average taller than the Nuggets—but they had a pair of star players in John Trimble and Kenny Lemay. Trimble was a quick, crafty grade nine point guard who was considered to be the best defender in the city. Lemay was a lanky grade eight small forward who could shoot the three-pointer better than almost anyone in the league.

"It's pretty simple. Contain these two guys and we should win," Coach Stephens told them. "But if we let Trimble get a bunch of steals and Lemay take a whole pile of open threes, we might as well just give up now because they will bury us. Does everybody understand this?"

Heads nodded solemnly all around. One of the best things about Coach Stephens was that he was meticulously prepared. He knew everything about the team South Side was facing, their strengths, their weaknesses and how best to take advantage of them. No Stinger could ever complain about being unprepared, at least not from a coaching standpoint.

"There's one other thing before we get to work," the coach continued. "We've had a bit of bad luck. Matt's right hand is worse today, not better. We're not sure if he's going to be able to play Friday. So we're going to have to prepare as though he's not.

"That means Phil Wong will take the point with the first team for practice. If Matt isn't able to go on Friday, I want Phil to feel as comfortable as possible. Matt, you watch from the sidelines for today, okay?"

Even though Matt knew it was coming, being taken out of the starting unit for practice almost hurt worse than the kick that Jackson had leveled at his hand. He glanced over at Phil, who seemed to be surprised by the coach's words. Phil had worked as hard as anybody and had earned the chance to play more minutes. And even though Matt was nearly sick about being on the sidelines himself, he had to feel good for Phil.

Matt moved over to the bleachers to watch the team begin running through the offense it would use against North Vale's aggressive man-to-man defense. But before he could sit down, Andrea called to him from the open door of the trainer's room. "Matt," she said. "Come in here."

He wasn't sure why, exactly, but Matt felt his cheeks flush and his hands grow sweaty as he made his way across the gym. Andrea was holding a couple of ice packs, some tape and a makeshift sling made out of cloth. "Coach said we need to ice this down for at least a half hour each day," she said. "I'll fix you up so the ice won't be slipping all over."

Matt watched as Andrea worked expertly with the tape and the sling to keep the ice in place. She seemed to enjoy the job, although for the life of him Matt couldn't understand why. Some of the players took what she did for granted, like she was some kind of slave to the team. But Matt had seen Andrea play soccer and even shoot hoops before she had been injured. She was a better athlete than many of the boys she now waited on hand and foot as a team manager.

"What do you do this for?" he asked her as she finished up the tape job. "I mean, what fun is this for you, anyway?"

"I don't know," Andrea replied, her eyebrows arching and her blue eyes growing wider. "It's just being around a team, you know. I just like the feeling. If it wasn't for my leg, I'd be playing hoops too. And I couldn't stand being the manager on the girls' team because it would be too hard to watch from the bench knowing I should be out there. Being manager with the boys lets me still be part of a team. Plus I think I might be interested in training or physiotherapy someday."

"You mean, like a career?" Matt asked.

"Maybe," Andrea said. "What do you want to do?"

"I don't know," Matt replied. He suddenly realized he hadn't given it a lot of serious thought. "NBA multi-millionaire superstar, I guess."

Andrea groaned and they both laughed. Matt hadn't talked much with her before this, even though they shared the same advisory period and every basketball practice. Andrea seemed pretty cool, though, and Matt found her easier to talk with than most of the girls he knew through school or the neighborhood. She seemed more normal and she liked sports. Obviously, Andrea also knew a thing or two about overcoming adversity.

Matt watched the rest of practice before heading home to meet his mom. As they drove to the clinic, he asked her, "Mom, what do you think I should do?"

"Well, you know I want you to see the doctor about it," she said. "Then, we'll have to decide..."

"No," Matt said, a little irritated. "I mean, what should I do? You know, like for a job, a career?"

"Oh," she said. "I didn't know you were thinking about that kind of stuff yet. I don't know, Matt. What are you interested in?"

"Well, sports," he said, grinning at her. "You know that, I guess. But I don't know what kind of job I could get in that area. Andrea was telling me today that she might want to be a trainer."

"Andrea?" his mom said, stifling the urge to smile. "I haven't heard you talk about Andrea. Is that the girl who helps out your coach?"

"Yeah," Matt replied. "She's our trainer. She gave me some ice for my hand."

After a minute examining Matt's right hand and asking him a few questions, Dr. Shaw delivered the news. "It's just a deep bruise, Matt," she said. "I know it's awfully sore. Just keep icing it for the rest of the week and take it easy. That's about all you can do."

"Can I play basketball?" Matt asked breathlessly.

"Give it a day or two," the doctor replied. "If the pain starts subsiding, you can decide for yourself if you're capable of playing."

chapter seventeen

It was the final practice of the season. Win or lose, after Friday's game the year was over. They would either finish as city champions or runners-up. And this Thursday session was their last run through the stretching, dribbling, defensive drills and offensive plays that had marked every one of Coach Stephens' highly organized practices since that first afternoon in September.

Everybody was excited about the big game, but probably nobody more than Matt. His right hand was still bruised, but the swelling had subsided and it was nowhere near as sore to the touch as it had been just a couple of days earlier. Matt had rejoined team workouts on Wednesday, and as he ran through the familiar warm-up drills with his teammates and the sweat began to trickle down his neck, he felt pretty close to normal again.

"Hill, you take first team today," Coach Stephens barked. Matt switched his reversible jersey over to the solid maroon color worn in practice by the starting unit, while Phil flipped his own jersey back to white. "Glad you're doing better," Phil said as he switched over to defense. "But you better be one hundred percent. I'm coming after you today."

Matt smiled. It was typical Phil. Matt knew that Phil would push him as hard as he possibly could during this final practise session.

The Stingers were all business as they steamed their way through practice. Six months of workouts and games had raised everybody's skill level, and day after day of practising together had made South Side a finely tuned unit. The ball zipped back and forth between the starting five as they worked it against the mock North Vale matchup zone being played by the second team. Everybody's confidence level was high. Matt could feel it growing by the minute.

"All right, bring it in," Coach Stephens said, motioning the players to gather where the giant hornet crest of the Stingers marked the tip-off circle.

"Tomorrow is the biggest day in each of your basketball careers so far. It's an important game, and one I think we have a good chance of winning. The gym will be packed and everybody will be making a big fuss out of the fact it's for the city championship.

"I know you guys will represent your school well. I have no doubt about that. Just remember two things: Give it your absolute best effort, and have fun. Tomorrow is one of those days in your lives that you'll always remember, even when you're forty-five-years-old and playing pickup ball at the YMCA. Trust me, I can remember every big game I played, even back when I was your age.

"Okay, hit the showers," the coach concluded. "We'll see you all at the pep rally tomorrow."

Matt wanted to make sure he was as well pre-pared as possible for the city final. So he iced his right hand for a half hour after supper, did his homework and then glanced at the clock radio on his bedroom dresser. It said 9:30. Time for bed, he decided. He would try to get as much sleep as he could tonight.

But going to sleep was much easier said than done. Matt kept running over the Stingers' offensive sets in his mind. He kept thinking about how he had to make sure to protect the ball against the hawk-ing defense of John Trimble. He thought about his damaged right hand and wondered if it would hold up to the physical intensity of a city final. He kept looking at the glowing digits on his clock, trying to will himself to sleep and growing more frustrated by the minute. It was past 10:30 before he finally nodded off.

The alarm sounded, waking Matt from a fitful sleep. But within a few seconds, he was in full motion. Nobody had to coax him out of bed this morning, not with the city championship game that afternoon.

Matt made his way downstairs to the kitchen. He had meticulously planned his routine the night before. His white home uniform with the maroon piping around the V-neck and the words "South Side" across the chest was ready in the dryer along with his socks and baggy white shorts. He folded them neatly and slid them into his gym bag along with the nearly pristine black and white hightop Air Jordans that he saved for indoor basketball.

Next he went to the kitchen cupboard, pulled out a bowl and some Raisin Bran and lined them up neatly on the counter top. He walked to the front door and grabbed the *Post* off the front step. Then he methodically munched down his cereal as he flipped the paper directly to the Sports section.

The first three pages were full of NBA and NHL scores and a preview of this weekend's NCAA Tournament third-round games. But on the fourth page, a small headline caught Matt's eye and quickened his pulse. In fact, he almost spit a mouthful of Raisin Bran across the page.

The headline appeared over a brief article in the section reserved for local sports news. "South Side–North Vale to clash in city final," it read.

"The top two middle school basketball teams in the city will square off this afternoon for the playoff championship," the article began.

"The South Side Stingers, led by grade nine center Dave Tanner, the city's top rebounder this year, earned homecourt advantage for the final by finishing first in the regular season. Bolstering the Stingers' chances considerably is the fact standout grade seven point guard Matthew Hill has recovered from a hand injury that had threatened to keep him off the court…"

Matt could hardly believe his eyes. His name was in the *Post*! And they had actually called him a "standout." That was the only mention of him in the article, but Matt was stunned and thrilled all at the same time. His heart was beating rapidly and his mind was racing. He just had to show his mom.

She was blow-drying her hair, getting ready for work, when Matt burst into her bedroom. "Look at this!" he shouted. "I made the paper. This is unreal."

Matt's mom carefully surveyed the story, a smile coming to her face as she read her son's name. "We'll have to save this and show Mark, won't we?" she beamed. "I'm very proud of you."

Matt was practically walking on air as he left for school. By the time he reached the big tree, Jake and Phil were already there, holding copies of the *Post*. "Can we get an autograph?" Phil joked. "Any comment, Matthew?" Jake laughed, poking fun at the fact the newspaper had used Matt's more formal full first name.

Matt was blushing as the three friends made their way to South Side. They were all excited about the game that afternoon and, as they approached the school, they realized they weren't alone. "City Finals Today," read the signboard at the corner of the parking lot near the entrance. "Go Stingers!"

Matt had never seen such a big deal being made about a game, at least not one in which he had ever played a part. Principal Walker even talked it up on the morning announcements, encouraging all the students to come out and support the team at the rally that afternoon.

At lunchtime, the cheerleaders and drill team staged the biggest pep rally of the school year, and many of the players' parents also attended. Matt was a little disappointed that his mom couldn't make it, but she was with out-of-town clients who had only one day in which to find and buy a house. He would much sooner have her at the game. "Whatever happens today, it's been a great season for Stingers basketball," Coach Stephens told the assembled students. "And I want to thank the student body for your support all season long."

Matt could barely concentrate through his afternoon classes. Somehow, math and English didn't seem too exciting with tip-off looming in less than two hours. But he managed to avoid constantly looking at the clock until late in the day. He glanced up near the end of social studies. It was 3:25. Almost time.

When the bell finally rang, Matt nearly flew to his locker. He threw his books inside, grabbed his gym bag and headed for the gymnasium. If there was any game for which proper preparation was important it was this one.

After Matt had carefully put on his uniform and his shoes—making sure, as usual, to tie the left before the right—he headed for the trainer's room. Andrea was waiting there for him, ready to wrap his right hand. She carefully wove bandaging around his outside knuckles, placing a cushioned pad on the underside of the wrap to give the injured spot maximum protection without getting in the way of his fingers. The wrap felt good as Matt picked up a basketball to give it a test dribble. If he hadn't seen the bandage on his hand, he probably wouldn't have even known it was there.

The hand felt great in warm-ups. Matt was able to catch and dribble and shoot with almost no discomfort. As he glanced down the floor at the North Vale Nuggets, who were warming up at the other end, he had a good feeling about this game. The crowd of about four hundred South Side students and parents, taking the lead from the cheerleading unit, obviously felt confident too. It was the most intense gymnasium atmosphere Matt had ever experienced.

As he looked down toward the North Vale bench, Matt noticed John Trimble, the Nuggets' point guard, talking with Grant Jackson, who was seated behind the North Vale bench. The two had been teammates on summer all-star teams and were obviously still friends.

Dave Tanner easily won the opening tip, flicking the ball back to Matt, who brought it up the floor. On this first possession, Tanner cut hard to the top of the key with his arms outstretched as if he was looking for a quick pass. Matt faked it and then lobbed the ball high inside to Tanner, who had reversed his stride and darted directly for the hoop. The result was an easy lay-up to start the game. South Side was already on a roll.

Matt couldn't ever remember feeling this comfortable on the basketball court. He was on fire too, hitting three of his first four shots as South Side moved out to an eight-point lead early in the second quarter. As Phil subbed in to give Matt a quick breather, he grinned at his buddy. "Good job, man. You're killing those guys."

Matt watched from the bench as Phil directed the offense. The Stingers' confidence was surging, spurred on by the electricity of the home crowd. By the time Matt returned to the game, with just five minutes left in the half, South Side had extended its lead to ten points.

On his first play back, Matt dribbled down the court, used a screen by Tanner to break free from his man and drained a rainbow three-pointer. It seemed everything he was shooting was going in. South Side managed a defensive stop and, the next time down the floor, Matt put a head-fake on Trimble and then blew by him for an easy scoop lay-up. The Stingers led by fifteen, Matt already had thirteen points, and the first half wasn't even over. He stole a glance into the stands above the South Side bench. His mom and Mark were watching intently. It felt great to be playing so well in front of both of them.

Matt was certainly in a zone, feeling like he could beat anybody, make any shot. Meanwhile, North Vale seemed to be disintegrating under the pressure of the championship game. Another Nuggets' turnover led to yet another Stingers' possession. Tanner set a sturdy screen for Matt and he went left around it, pulling up again for a jumper. But before he could get off the shot, John Trimble's right arm swung down hard on Matt's shooting hand, chopping him across the bandage covering the injured knuckles. The basketball popped loose, the whistle blew and the referee signaled for Matt to go to the free-throw line.

But within seconds, Matt knew that was going to be impossible. The foul by Trimble hadn't been dirty, but it had been hard enough to do some serious damage. Matt clenched the bandaged portion of his right hand, the searing pain causing him to move it up and down in a rocking motion.

The hand hurt far worse than it had even a week before when Grant Jackson had kicked him. He could feel the knuckles swelling under the bandage. Matt looked at Coach Stephens on the bench. He didn't have to say anything. "Time-out," the coach yelled at the referee. "We've got a player hurt."

Coach Stephens ran out onto the floor. "It's the same hand, isn't it?" he asked. Matt nodded. "Come on over to the bench."

Matt found a spot on the bench and stuck out his arm so Andrea could place an ice pack on it. The referee ran over to where Coach Stephens was sitting. "That's your shooter, Coach," he said pointing to Matt. "Do you want to sub for him since he's injured?"

"Well, he can't shoot," the coach replied. "Yeah, we'll sub."

"Phil!" the coach yelled down the bench. "You're in for Matt and you're shooting free throws."

Phil bounced off the bench and quickly stripped off his warm-ups. He jogged to the line. It was difficult, coming in off the bench cold to shoot free throws and

Phil looked nervous. His first shot was off right and it bounced harmlessly away from the rim.

"One shot," the referee said.

This time, Phil swished the free throw. South Side led by sixteen with just three minutes left in the first half. Matt had a strong feeling he wasn't going back into this game. The pain in his hand told him that he wouldn't be able to use it for awhile. But the team looked to be in good shape to win the city title, even without him on the floor.

North Vale called a time-out following Phil's free throw. When they emerged from their huddle, it was clear they had changed their defense, picking up their Stingers' checks full-court. Matt knew what was coming. The Nuggets had thrown on a full-court press, hoping to take advantage of Phil, a new and less experienced ball handler, being in the game.

The visitors' strategy worked. Phil was a cautious ball handler and not as quick as Matt. Trimble was all over him and, on three of the next four possessions, Phil turned over the ball. By halftime, North Vale had narrowed the Stingers' lead to just ten points. Nobody in the South Side gym seemed too comfortable anymore.

In the locker room, Matt felt horrible. Doctor Taylor, who volunteered his services during South Side home games, came in and checked out his right hand, gently squeezing the injured knuckles and probing the wrist and fingers as well. "There's a chance you've got a small break in a bone here, Matt," he said. "We'll have to get an X-ray this weekend, but you certainly won't be playing anymore today. Make sure you keep the ice bag on it."

Matt had known in his heart that he wouldn't be going back on the court. But having the doctor spell it out for him was nevertheless difficult to hear. His teammates were disappointed too. It wasn't like they didn't have confidence in Phil, but Matt had been the starting point guard ever since Jackson had been kicked off the team.

Phil sat in his stall, looking tense. Bringing up the ball against a grade nine like Trimble, in the pressure of a city championship game, was a tall order for a grade seven who had spent most of his season on the bench. But Matt knew that nobody would give it a better effort than his buddy would.

"Guys, we have a ten-point lead and just one half to play," Coach Stephens said. "But this half won't be easy. This Nuggets team is tough. Just go out there and do your best. That is always good enough, no matter the result."

The team met in the middle of the locker room and each extended his right hand into the huddle. Matt stuck in his good left hand instead. "One, two, three—Stingers!" they yelled. No matter what happened over the next twenty minutes, this was one of the last such cheers of the season. That sudden realization made Matt sad.

The Nuggets continued where they had left off in the first half. They clamped on the full-court press and nearly gave Phil fits as he tried to work the ball upcourt. Coach Stephens eventually brought Dave Tanner into the backcourt to give Phil some help and that solved the problem. But in the meantime, the Stingers' lead had slipped away. And with just twenty-nine seconds left in the game, South Side found itself trailing, for the first time, by two points.

Coach Stephens called a time-out to set up the Stingers' next play. It was an important one. A miss on this possession and the game could be over.

"Okay, guys," the coach said intently. "I'm setting up this play for Phil. He's one of the best three-point shooters in the city, and now is the time for us to use that weapon."

The coach drew up a play: Phil would bring the ball downcourt, pass to Tanner at the top of the key and then cut through the paint and around a low screen set up by Pete Winters. "He'll be open after he clears that screen, okay Dave?" the coach said. "Get him the ball where he can shoot it."

Coach Stephens turned his attention to Phil. "Just make sure you get the shot up with at least five seconds left on the clock, okay? That will give us time for a rebound, not that we're going to need it, Phil," he smiled. "You're money from three. You can do this."

The players broke the huddle with their customary "Stingers!" chant reverberating through the now strangely quiet gym. Matt watched nervously as his teammates took the floor without him. He was a little surprised that coach had called the play for Phil, who had struggled since entering the game after Matt's injury. He had expected the ball to go to steady senior Dave Tanner, who was playing his last game for South Side, or to Amar, who had already scored eighteen points and had completely dominated his defender. But the move was smart, Matt realized. Nobody on the North Vale bench would expect Phil to take the final shot. It was a gutsy call and just the sort of quirky strategy that Coach Stephens had become known for over the years.

Phil brought the ball downcourt, closely checked by Trimble. The North Vale guard made a lunge for the ball near the top of the free-throw circle and Phil, hitching his dribble slightly, almost turned it over. But he managed to recover his balance in time to plant firmly and toss a hard pass to Tanner in the high post. Phil then cut quickly through the key toward the spot where Winters was to set the screen. The play worked like a charm. Trimble hadn't expected the sudden cut by Phil and he was left in the dust.

Phil broke free to the corner and was wide open

when Tanner delivered the ball with just six seconds remaining on the clock. On the bench, Matt's heart was beating so fast he could hardly breathe as he watched the play unfold. Phil caught the pass with his feet set squarely behind the three-point line, just as Matt had seen his buddy do so many times on the Anderson Park courts.

Phil released the ball and it traveled on a flawless arc toward the basket, cleanly swishing through the mesh and onto the floor. Before Trimble could gather the ball and inbound it, the final buzzer sounded. South Side had won the city championship and Phil had made the final shot.

Matt felt himself being pushed by a wave of sweaty teammates onto the floor as they homed in on Phil, who was looking both stunned and elated at the same time, as if he hardly believed what had just happened. In seconds, he was buried in a pile of maroon and white uniforms as the Stingers mobbed their unlikely late-game hero.

By the time a widely smiling Phil emerged from the pile, his uniform and his black hair were uncharacteristically askew. Matt had avoided the pile because of his injured hand, but he rushed up to his friend. "Phil it up! Phil it up!" he yelled, barely able to contain himself. "You are so clutch!"

The two teams lined up at center court to shake hands, Matt extending his uninjured left to each of the Nuggets. When he met John Trimble near the end of the line, the North Vale star stopped him. "Sorry about the foul," Trimble said earnestly. "I don't care what Jackson says, you can play. You were killing me before you got hurt. Nice game."

The praise meant a lot to Matt as he headed for the locker room. In the excitement, he had almost forgotten about his hand. The satisfied feeling he got when he saw Dave Tanner and Pete Winters celebrating a city title in their last year of middle school was more than enough to dull the pain. And the joy on Phil's face, the hero in the locker room who was busy answering questions from a *Post* reporter, made everything, including the hand, seem okay.

Matt looked around the room at his closest buddies—Jake, Amar and Phil. They had all come so far and had made such huge improvements since the start of this year. Matt remembered back to September and how they had each just hoped to make the team. Only a few months ago, Jake and Phil had walked slowly out of this very gym, crushed at not making the varsity. Now all four of them were city champions, and they were already making their mark on the proud tradition of South Side basketball. Best of all, they were doing it together, just like always.

Suddenly, all the adjustments to middle school, the problems with Grant Jackson, the troubles at Wong's Grocery, the suspension and the injury faded to the background. The bass was pounding out of Dave Tanner's stereo system and even Coach Stephens couldn't help boogying a little as he made his way from stall to stall to high five each of his players. Matt stared down at his right hand, wondering if it was broken or just badly bruised again. Right at this moment, he had to admit, it didn't really seem to matter.

Jeff Rud has worked as a journalist for the Victoria *Times Colonist* for the past twenty years. He currently covers provincial politics for the newspaper, working out of the British Columbia legislature. This is Rud's fourth book and first fiction effort. The 44-year-old lives in Victoria with his wife Lana, a middle school teacher, and their two young children. His favorite pastime is playing pick up basketball.